THE BLOW-IN

SUSANNE O'LEARY

Copyright©2016 by Susanne O'Leary

This book is a work of fiction. The names, characters, places and incidents either are products of the writer's imagination or are used fictitiously. Any resemblance to actual persons living or dead, actual events, locales, or organizations is entirely coincidental.

All rights reserved. With the exception of quotes used in reviews, no portion of this book may be reproduced, used, or transmitted in any form or by any means without written permission from the author.

This is a work of fiction. Names, characters, places, brands, media, and incidents are either the products of the author's imagination or are used factiously. The author acknowledges the trademarked status and trademark owners of various products of various products referenced in this work of fiction, which have been used without permission. The publications/use of these trademarks is not authorized, associated with, or sponsored by the trademark owners

Cover design and typesetting by J.D. Smith Design

CHAPTER 1

Resigning as top reporter from Ireland's biggest newspaper in the middle of a corruption scandal that had made the headlines all over the world must have been the strangest career move ever. Why didn't I stay and cash in on the glory and all that publicity? Why didn't I write yet another book and make even more money than with the first one? Those were the questions people kept asking me, and I refused to answer. Simply because I couldn't. Except that it had to do with something outdated called integrity and honour. Mine and Maureen's, my then best friend and boss. We both resigned from the newspaper in an act of defiance, giving the finger to the establishment and their powers of persuasion. That gesture gave us a momentary buzz that was hard to beat.

The euphoria was swiftly replaced by a plunge into depression and binge drinking. Maureen retreated into her private life, learning to play golf and bridge, and looking after her daughters. But I had no family or even a love interest to cuddle up to. I was all alone with my regrets.

It wasn't until my brother stepped back into my life that I woke up and took a good look at myself.

Seamus towered above me as I lay on the sofa flicking the remote.

"What are you *doing*, Finola?" he thundered.

"Watching TV," I mumbled from the depths of the cushions.

"It isn't even on."

"Nothing worth watching."

"Why are you still in your pyjamas at five o'clock?"

"Not going anywhere."

Seamus took a deep breath. "Jesus, Finola, you have to wake up and get out of that pit you're in. You have to eat."

"I do."

"All I could find in your fridge was half a bottle of vodka and a lemon. What do you call that?"

I shrugged. "Dunno. Dinner?"

He sat down beside me and pulled me up. "I'm worried about you. Sharon is, too."

"Sharon? Worried? That must be the first time ever."

"I know you two don't get on. But that's because you're so different."

"That's the understatement of the year," I muttered.

"She wants to help."

"How? By giving me a make-over?" Sharon, Seamus's wife, was a personal shopper at Brown Thomas, Dublin's answer to Harvey Nichols, the department store where even the air was expensive.

"She said she'd treat you to a spa weekend."

I let out a hollow laugh. "She just wants to turn me into a girl."

He put his arm around me. "Would that be so bad?"

I sighed and put my head on his shoulder. Good old Seamus, my brother and comrade-in-arms as we grew up. We stuck together as our parents battled with each other, whimpered behind the sofa as our dad hurled drunken insults at our mother and helped each other and Mum when Dad died of a heart attack and we finally had peace. But Seamus stayed at home while I went out into the world to carve out a career as a hot-shot journalist. And look at us now. He, the solid, dependable accountant, and me, burnt out after my recent battles against corruption and dishonesty in the world of politics. Yes, I'd won, but the victory cost more than I could afford.

"Will you do it?" he asked. "For me?"

"What?"

"Go on that spa weekend with Sharon. Get yourself sorted. Stop drinking. Eat healthy food. Brush your hair and tidy yourself up a bit."

I pulled away and noticed the concern in his eyes. "Okay. I will."

He hugged me. "Thank you, Finola. I know it'll be hard. But you'll feel so much better in the end."

"Yeah, sure. A massage and facial cure all ills." But I got up and gave him a hug. "This will hurt me more than it'll hurt you."

It did hurt at first. Pulling myself together to take a shower was the first step. Looking in the mirror the second. I was not a pretty sight. Sharon was facing a huge challenge.

But she rose to it. Beautifully. Like a sergeant major pushing a new recruit through a drill, she dragged me to the spa hotel, where I was put through an agonising form of torture known as a 'full body and face restoration programme'. I suffered through it all without complaining, even when the hairdresser cut my hair short and asked what colour I wanted the highlights.

"Purple," I said in defiance. But as the dye seeped into my scalp, I had second thoughts. My hair had always been auburn. I was a woman with auburn hair. But when I saw the result, I was quite happy. The purple highlights were subtle and the short hair made me look funky. But whatever. Who cared what I looked like, anyway?

I slept for fourteen hours after that weekend and woke up feeling and looking annoyingly sparkly.

I looked at the shiny new me in the mirror.

"Holy shit, I'm a girl," I said to myself, knowing this would only last a week or so if I didn't stick to the healthy routine Sharon had drawn up for me. But hey, it was worth it. I didn't know a purple tinge to my hair would suit me so well or that my skin could be this rosy. I was beginning to look quite attractive, which gave me a little spark of something new. Not drinking was hard and not bingeing on pizza, harder. My fridge was full of healthy stuff like broccoli and salad. I was drinking water as if I'd spent a week in the desert. And I was feeling weirdly energetic. I was even considering looking for a job.

But what kind of job? No newspaper in Dublin would hire me. I was too much trouble, too much of a risk. I might as well have tattooed 'rebel' across my forehead. No editor wanted that. But did I really want to go back to my old job? I asked myself. Did I even want to stay in Dublin? Or in this country? I was thinking of looking for something in the US when I got a tip from a journalist friend.

"How about applying for the editor job that has just come up in County Tipperary?" he asked over a coffee in Temple Bar one dreary Tuesday in late April.

"Tipperary? But I thought I might go somewhere foreign," I said.

"It would be," he quipped. "If you compare it to Dublin, I mean. It's the real country, Finola. I bet you've never even been there."

"Yes I have. I went to see the Rock of Cashel with my parents when I was ten."

"I didn't mean Tipperary per se, I meant the *country*. As in small villages, farms, fields, cows and horses."

"Oh God." I shuddered. "I'm a city girl. The countryside scares me."

"It'll be good for you. A break from everything. And you could do something fun, like a blog about city life versus country life. 'The confessions of a city slicker' or something like that." He fiddled with his phone. "I have the details here. I'll email them to you and you can take a look."

"Okay, thanks," I said, thinking I'd delete the email as soon as I got it. Moving to the country seemed more alien than taking up a job in Kazakhstan. But a phone call from Sharon changed my mind.

"There's a big sale at Kildare Village," she said. "All kinds of designer stuff going for half price. You could get yourself some bargains there."

"Thanks," I said through gritted teeth. "But I'm not really into clothes and make-up."

"Oh, come on, let's go and have a look at least. It'll be fun. I have the day off on Monday, and you're not working. I'm dying to update your wardrobe. And then we can go to the Benefit shop where they demonstrate their great new line in make-up. We can have lunch at that new French place after shopping. I've already told my friend and her brother we're coming. He wants to meet you."

I knew instantly what she was up to. "Well, you'll have to tell them I won't be there."

"Where will you be?" Sharon sounded annoyed.

"Away. I'm going off to…find myself."

"Oooh." I could nearly see the wheels turning in her brain. "I see. A mindfulness course, is it?"

"Something like that," I said airily. "You know, like a detox for the mind."

"I see. Well, give us a shout when you're back."

"I will," I promised.

Everything happened very fast after that. I contacted the newspaper in Cloughmichael, County Tipperary, and set up a job interview for the following week. Not knowing if I'd get the job, I stuck my neck out and contacted a rental agency, who would let my apartment until further notice, packed my bags, loaded them into my trusty Mini Cooper Roadster and set off for the wilds of County Tipperary.

A long way to go. In more ways than one.

* * *

"Finola McGee, editor-in-chief," it said on the gleaming brass plate.

I picked up my phone to take a shot of this amazing sight but put it back in my bag. No reason to celebrate or brag about it. Had it been The Irish Telegraph, where I had been the political reporter until recently, it would have been a big deal. But it was a tiny local rag in a little town in County Tipperary with a circulation of about four thousand. A bit of a come-down it would seem. But, ah well, I was taking a break from the hustle and bustle—to rest and recuperate among the rolling hills and green valleys of the Irish countryside. To breathe fresh air. To listen to the birds in the early morning. To enjoy silence, calm and bucolic country life. Running the Knockmealdown News would be fun and different, I told myself. I might even find myself a handsome farmer to marry and have five kids and a dog. My mother would be beside herself with joy.

"Why Knockmealdown?" I wondered when I applied for the job.

"Because of the mountain range," Jerry Murphy, the owner and publisher told me during the job interview in his local pub, pointing out the window as he downed a pint of Guinness with impressive speed.

"Of course," I said, feeling stupid as I looked out over the green slopes of said mountains. "I should have realised."

Jerry nodded and raised a finger, which resulted in a waiter racing across the grubby carpet, coming to a screeching halt at our table like The Road Runner. I was impressed. I usually had to grab waiters by their throats to get them to take any notice.

"Another one, please, Paddy," Jerry said. "How about you,

Finola? Will you join me in a pint? They pull the best one in Ireland here."

Mentally salivating at the thought of a well-pulled pint of the black stuff, I toyed with my glass of Ballygowan. But the new me only drank alcohol at weekends.

"No thanks. I'll stick to water."

He studied me with his bird-like pale-blue eyes. "You're not a pioneer, are you?"

I faked a jolly laugh. "Not at all. I do like a pint now and then. But…" I hesitated. "I gave it up for lent."

"It's the end of May."

"It's a kind of detox thing."

He eyed my bag of bacon crisps. "Right. Okay. Just the one then, Paddy," he said to the waiter, a tall man with teeth like a horse.

"Righty-o, Jerry," Paddy chortled and prepared to leave.

Jerry stopped him. "Before you go, I'd like you to meet our new editor."

Paddy's eyes widened as he noticed me. "Jesus Christ, if it isn't Finola McGee." He wiped his hand on the back of his trousers and grabbed mine in an iron grip. "The famous Finola!"

"How did you know?" I asked, trying not to wince.

"I've seen you on the telly a couple of times. No mistaking that freckly face and the wild hair. Except now it's short and purple. Suits you."

"Thanks."

"It's an honour to meet you. You sure know how to wipe the floor with them politicians. Good on ya, Finola."

I eased my hand out of his grip. "That's all in the past, Paddy."

"In the past?" Paddy looked deflated. "You mean you're not going to dig up the dirt of the goings-on in the local County Council? Or make a bit of a stir during the election campaign?"

I glanced at Jerry. "Not really. I'm taking a bit of a sabbatical. I've had enough of politicians."

Paddy rolled his eyes. "Haven't we all? Anyway, it's great to meet you, Finola. I'll get that pint for you, Jerry." Paddy picked up the empty pint glass and disappeared.

Jerry turned back to me. "So, there you go. You've got the job."

I smiled. "I kind of figured that out about ten minutes ago. But thanks. I'm looking forward to working with you."

He nodded and ran his hand over his sparse black hair. "I won't interfere with you a lot. As long as you stick to what you just said, you're free to run the paper on your own."

"What I just said?" I tried to remember if I'd said anything about how I'd run the paper.

He nodded. "That thing about not digging around in the affairs of politicians." He leaned forward and fixed his eyes on me. "The Knockmealdown News is just that—news. We stick to facts and leave the rest alone. I know you've solved crimes, exposed corruption and got people arrested and convicted. But we don't want sensationalism. This paper was started by my great-grandfather in eighteen eighty-five. We've weathered some pretty bad storms all through the nineteen sixteen rising, the civil war, the troubles and the recent austerity, and still kept going. It's a paper our readers trust and enjoy. We've kept a positive, feel-good vibe. And that's the way we want to continue." He drew breath and took a long pull of the pint Paddy had just placed by his elbow.

"So, by keeping your head under the blanket, you stayed out of trouble?" I couldn't help asking.

His eyes turned cold. "We're *neutral*."

"I see."

"There will be no 'Finola Reveals' in this paper," he continued. "I hope you understand."

"Absolutely," I said, taken aback by the fire in his eyes. "I've left all that kind of reporting behind. I just want to enjoy country life and get to know everyone around here. I don't have the energy to stir up trouble anymore."

He leant back. "Good. I have to confess I hesitated when I saw you'd applied for the job. But then my wife told me not to be a wimp. 'If you can get Finola McGee, grab her,' she said. She was a huge fan of your column. She thinks you can give us a push by updating the paper a bit. 'Sexing it up,' she said, but that was after a few glasses of wine. I decided to hire you despite my slight hesitation. Well, we needed someone fast, as our last editor left suddenly for…health reasons."

I was going to ask him to elaborate, but his face had that closed look that meant he wasn't going to say anything else.

As I stood there, admiring the brass plaque on the door of my new office, I wondered why my predecessor had left. I didn't know much about him, only that he'd been the editor-in-chief for twenty years but had then resigned, leaving no forwarding address. Strange career move. But who was I to talk?

CHAPTER 2

My first day at the paper was spent getting my bearings and meeting the staff. More like a skeleton staff, I found. It appeared that each of the five or so people who worked at the office in the old Georgian pile at the edge of town wore several hats. My office, a cavernous space that had once been the drawing room, still had the original sash windows, parquet flooring and period fireplace. A huge mahogany desk was placed at the far end with an old leather armchair behind it. Spindly dining-room chairs were scattered on the old Donegal carpet, the once-vivid colours faded by sunlight and time. Not quite the dusty old office I expected, but this town was full of surprises. I wondered how the paper was run.

All was revealed by a pudgy baby-faced young man called Dan O'Meara, who appeared in my office only minutes after I'd arrived.

"Hello, Ms McGee," he panted, having run up the winding staircase to the first floor. "I'm Dan O'Meara. The reporter, like." He smoothed his thatch of brown hair and held out a beefy hand.

"Hi, Dan." I got up from behind the desk and shook his hand. "Please, call me Finola."

He blushed. "Okay, thanks, er, Finola. I'm a huge fan. I used to read your column every week, like. Finola Reveals was the best part of The Irish Telegraph. "

"Thank you. That's very kind. *The* reporter, you said?"

He nodded. "Yes. I'm the only real reporter, like. Mary does the layout and handles advertising, Fidelma covers sport, country fairs, the local hunt ball and whatever the parishes are up to, like. Both the Protestant and Catholic. Annie does weddings and funerals and runs the family section, and all the rest. And then there's Sinead on the switchboard." He drew breath.

"What about you?"

He looked confused for a second. "Me? Oh, well, I do everything else. All the real reporting. Crime, politics, gossip and so on, like. I mean, we'll do that together. You and me, I mean."

"I see. Is there a resident photographer?"

"Yes. Me."

I burst out laughing. "I've arrived in the land of multi-tasking."

He shrugged. "Yeah, well. It works, like."

"Do you say like at the end of every sentence?" I felt compelled to ask.

He squirmed. "No. Well…only when I'm nervous, li—" He stopped, gulped and laughed. "I'll try to cut it out."

"I'd appreciate it. And the paper is published twice a week?" I breezed on.

He nodded. "Yes. On Thursdays and Saturdays, which means Wednesdays and Fridays are our busiest days."

"They would be. As today is Monday, we'll be setting up Thursday's edition. I've had a look at last week's paper, and I feel there's a lot to be done. Jerry said something about sexing—I mean updating the look of the paper."

Dan nodded, looking suddenly business-like. "Yes. He told me you would. He was running things since John Keegan left last month, but now you're here we can implement a few new ideas."

"New ideas?" I sat down behind the desk and switched on my laptop. "You have any?"

"Uh, yes. One or two."

"Please, Dan, sit down. You make me nervous standing there like Big Bird."

He let out another nervous laugh, pulled out one of the antique chairs and lowered his heavy frame onto the silk-covered seat. "Jerry never let me sit. He thought I'd break the chairs."

"You probably will. I'm going to ask Jerry if we could change the furniture to something more modern. This stuff must have been here for the past two hundred years. It has to be updated." I ran my hand over the smooth mahogany. "Except the desk. I love this desk." I propped my chin on my hand. "Anyway, let me have your ideas."

"Oh, um…well, first of all, I think you have to introduce yourself. To the readers, I mean. A lot of people will be very excited when they learn you're going to run our paper."

"Introduce myself? But if they already know who I am. Why do I need to?"

"They might have a lot of preconceived ideas. And some might even think you're stuck up and snooty because you're from Dublin. They could even suspect you're here to make trouble or something—which you're not, of course."

"No, certainly not," I said with feeling. "I'm here to enjoy country life, not sneer at it."

"Exactly." Dan was looking a lot more confident. "I thought that if we did something fun, like an interview, you'd have an opportunity to tell everyone why you're here and what you plan to do and so on."

"Nah, not an interview. That's so last year."

"Okay. How about something like 'Finola's Last Reveal' as a headline, and then it would be Ten Things You Didn't Know About Finola on page two. Short and snappy."

"Hmm." I leaned back in the creaking leather chair and put my hands behind my head, staring out the window while I thought.

Dan squirmed. "But if that's not a good idea, I could just draw up a bio and put it on the second page."

I turned back to him. "You know what, Dan?"

He nibbled at a fingernail. "Yes?"

"That's an excellent idea."

His face went pink. "Gee. Thanks."

I gazed at him for a moment. "Just out of interest, do you know why Johnny Keegan left?"

Dan looked at his hands. "Um, no, not really. I think he'd just had enough of the job. Or something," he ended.

"Something, huh?" I said. But I didn't press him on the matter. I had an odd feeling about the whole thing, but it was better not to dig around too much. Sleeping dogs and all that.

* * *

A woman with a cheery voice called later that day. "Hi, Finola," she said. "My name's Miranda. I'm Jerry's wife."

I put down my mug of tea. "Hi, Miranda. What can I do for you?"

"Nothing," she laughed. "Except to come to dinner tonight. I know it's short notice and all that, but I'm dying to meet you."

"Well, my social calendar is a complete blank, so yes, I'd love to."

"Great. I've invited a few of the local hunks who'll want to ogle you up close."

"Sounds scary."

"Don't worry. They're pretty civilised. We live in the old house next door to the Protestant church. Used to be the rectory. Seven okay?"

"Perfect."

"Great. It's casual. No need to dress up. See you then." Miranda hung up.

No need to dress up? I couldn't if my life depended on it. My current wardrobe consisted of three pairs of jeans in various states of repair, the newest being the dress-up pair. Shoes? Boots, runners and furry slippers. Tops? A black polo neck, a cream ditto, two blue shirts, a long-sleeved tee shirt and two woolly sweaters for cold days. A rain mac and a navy trouser suit I wore for posher affairs like press conferences and the odd reception had made their way into my suitcase as well. The rest of my clothes were in two boxes in Sharon's spare room.

As there was a chill in the air after heavy rain, I opted for the black polo neck, the dress-up pair of jeans and my boots that were fairly new and would look good with a polish. I buffed them up with a little spit on a piece of toilet paper. Unused to make-up, I still applied the foundation, mascara and blusher they'd handed out as a free sample at the spa. I brushed my hair that was still quite short and stepped back, looking at myself in the spotty mirror in my bedroom at the B and B. Not bad, I decided. In fact, I looked unusually clean and tidy with just a dash of glamour.

I giggled to myself, wondering what Shannon would think of the transformation of Finola McGee and picked up my phone to take my first ever selfie. Wherever she was, I'd swish this over to her by email. She and Paul could have a good laugh, lying in a hammock under a palm tree in Tahiti—or wherever they were on their round-the-world trip. I suddenly missed Shannon and the fun we had sleuthing together, hot on the trail of those cheating politicians. Those sure were the days.

But that was then and this was now. I was starting a brand new career as the editor of a country newspaper. Not an easy transformation but something I wanted to do and do well. I had come a long way since Seamus hauled me out of the sofa. I was ready for the next challenge.

I picked up my bag and headed out the door. Local hunks had better watch out.

* * *

Miranda Murphy looked exactly like a woman called Miranda should—dark ringlets, huge brown eyes, rings on her fingers and, possibly, bells on her toes. Dressed in a floor-length multi-coloured kaftan and a multitude of beads, she was gorgeous, weird and utterly loveable. The only mystery was why this beautiful creature had married a man like Jerry.

She flung the door open before I had a chance to ring the bell.

"Finola!" she panted and pulled me into a dim hall with a stone-flagged floor and mahogany wall panelling. When she hugged me tight, I breathed in spices and exotic flowers before she pulled back and stared at me.

"You're pretty. No, you're…handsome." She nodded. "Yes. That's what you are. A handsome woman."

"Um, thanks. And thanks for inviting me." I handed her my offering—a box of Roses chocolates I picked up at a petrol station on the way to the house. "Sorry. This was all I could find."

Miranda grabbed the box. "Aw, you shouldn't have. I love these. Full of sugar and crap but the best with a cup of tea around eleven a.m."

I relaxed. Miranda had a self-contained non-threatening quality that was very soothing.

"I love them too," I said. "Belgian chocolates and all that, but give me a box of Roses on a dull day and I'll scoff the lot."

Miranda let out a laugh like silver bells. "Me too." She hung up my leather jacket and put her arm through mine. "Let's go and have a chat before everyone arrives."

I checked my watch. "Am I early? Thought you said seven."

"I did. But nobody arrives on time around here. I always

say seven, knowing everyone will be here around eight. But don't worry. Dinner won't be ruined. Moroccan lamb stew. It's been in the Aga all day, so it should survive another half hour."

"Aga," I said, nearly tasting the stew. "I love the way all houses have these stoves around here."

"I couldn't live without mine. It's the great, big, throbbing heart of the house." Miranda walked ahead into a big room. Two big sofas upholstered in green velvet flanked the fireplace, where blazing logs mixed with sods of turf cast a cosy glow on the oak floor covered in colourful rugs. She turned to me. "Sit down. I'll get you a drink. What would you like? Paddy's or wine?"

"Oh, er…" I replied, thinking that as it was neither Saturday nor Sunday, I shouldn't have been drinking anything alcoholic. "Maybe just some water?"

Miranda peered at me. "Water? You're not a Protestant, are you?"

I laughed and sank down into the soft velvet cushions. "With a name like McGee?"

"I thought not. I have nothing against Protestants. After all, I am one myself. It's just that they can be so fecking puritanical. You're a teetotaller, then?"

"No, it's just a…well…I'm kind of trying to cut down. No drinking during the working week. That kind of thing."

Miranda looked relieved. "Oh. I see. But it's a party. I mean…would you not relax your rules just once in a while?"

I hesitated. Why be a party pooper? I wasn't driving, and a ten-minute walk would get me back to the B and B. "Well…now that you put it that way, why not? I'll have a glass of red, then."

"Brilliant. I'll go and get the wine, and Jerry. He was getting the kids organised with their homework upstairs, but he should have finished by now." She padded out of the room, yelling, "Jerry! Finola's here. Get yer arse downstairs!"

I couldn't help laughing at the sudden switch from sweet and gentle. Miranda was a hoot. I sat there staring into the fire enjoying the calm before what might be a storm, when Jerry walked into the room.

He held out his hand. "Hi, Finola. Thank you for coming so early."

I struggled from the soft embrace of the sofa and shook his hand. "Hi, Jerry. Thanks for inviting me. I didn't know I was early. But being on time is probably a city thing."

"Yeah, I'm sure it is. Here, we're lucky if anyone arrives before midnight. How about a drink? Or are you still on the dry?"

"No. Miranda's getting me some wine."

"Oh, great." He walked to the drinks trolley and poured himself a whiskey. In a soft blue sweater and jeans, he looked more relaxed and a lot younger than during that job interview at the pub.

"How many children do you have?" I asked.

"Three. All boys. Quite a handful, but Miranda's the one who cracks the whip. They're scared shitless of her and think I'm real pushover. Which is true. I find it hard to lay down the law, especially with our eldest. He's fourteen and getting into that monosyllabic grumpy stage." Jerry sighed. "We have tough times ahead."

"Tough times?" Miranda said as she came in carrying a tray with two bottles and glasses. "Here, Jerry, put these on the table and pour Finola and me a glass of red. Then we can say cheers and thank you for saving us from disaster."

"Disaster?" I took the glass from Jerry.

Miranda waved her glass of red in the air. "Yes. When Johnny left so suddenly without a word, Jerry had to step in and run the paper while all hell broke loose here, and the publishing business was in danger of going down the toilet. Plus two of the kids came down with chickenpox, and I had to put everything with the farm on hold to help out."

"Publishing? I asked, confused. "You mean Jerry publishes books as well as the newspaper? And a farm?"

Miranda sank down on the sofa and patted a cushion. "Come here and sit. I'll tell you all about it…us."

I sat down beside her. She was halfway through telling me about Jerry's publishing house in nearby Cashel and her own small organic vegetable and fruit farm, when Jerry interrupted her.

He sat down beside me, nursing his drink. "I think we need to tell Finola about the real disaster we're facing."

Miranda nodded. "Yes. I was building up to that."

I looked from one to the other. "What real disaster?"

"The paper's in trouble." Jerry downed his shot of whiskey in one go. "The bank's threatening to foreclose on the big loan we took out five years ago. It's been a struggle to meet the repayments. Then Johnny left, and even if we miss him, it gave us an opportunity to get someone—you—to breathe some life into the paper and help us increase our circulation."

"Oh my God," I stammered. "I had no idea."

"Sorry to spring this on you like that. We need to double our circulation. At least."

I stared at him. "That's a pretty tall order."

"But you did it with The Irish Telegraph," Miranda argued.

I nodded. "Yes, but that was because of all the scandals and my column. I can't do that here."

"Maybe you can do something else?" Jerry suggested. "Rejig the layout, report more news. Interview some of the important people who live around here, like the racehorse trainers, and get them to talk a bit about their private lives or something."

"How about a health-and-fitness section?" Miranda cut in. "And some kind of fun column by Finola about a city slicker dealing with country life, maybe?"

"Fashion," Jerry said. "Music, movies, we never did any of those things."

"I thought you told me to keep my head down and run the paper the traditional way," I remarked, my head spinning.

Jerry squirmed. "I know. But I've changed my mind. We have to shake things up or we'll die."

Miranda put her hand on my arm. "Finola, you're our only hope."

I closed my eyes for a second. This was heavy. Jerry and Miranda were facing ruin if I didn't pull out all the stops and more than doubled the circulation of The Knockmealdown News.

I opened my eyes and took a deep breath. "You know, guys, that's a very tough professional challenge you've thrown me. But…"

"But—?" Jerry and Miranda said in unison.

I beamed at them. "But what the hell, I'll give it my best shot."

Jerry let out a long sigh as if he'd been holding his breath for about half an hour. "Thank God for that."

I gave him a stern look. "But no breathing down my neck, okay? I don't want you to butt in on what I'm going to do."

Jerry held up his hand in a scout's-honour salute. "Absolutely. I officially give you a free hand. Do whatever you want to make the paper the talk of the town."

I grinned. "You might be sorry you said that." I lifted my glass. "Here's to The Knockmealdown News and the new look."

Miranda clinked her glass against mine. "Cheers to that."

Then the door burst open, and three men arrived pulling her out of the sofa and covering her with kisses. "Miranda!" they shouted. "Gorgeous Miranda!"

More people arrived, and suddenly the room was a cacophony of voices and laughter. The party was in full swing. I was pulled forward and introduced to a Mick and a Pat and a Siobhan and other assorted people who kept pouring in the door. I can't say all of them greeted me with enthusiasm. I got some limp handshakes and a polite "Hello, how are ya?" here and there, but that was all.

"They're a little bit nervous about meeting such a celebrity," Miranda whispered in my ear. "But let's get them some booze and they'll relax. We'll sit down in a minute, anyway, as soon as Rory arrives."

"Rory?"

"That's the farmer I rent my fields from. Rory Quirke. He's been over the hill with a mare today, so he said he might be late."

"Over the hill with a—?" I asked, when a tall man walked in.

He went straight over to Miranda and kissed her on the cheek. "Sorry, sweetheart. I just managed to unload the mare and change. That bastard, Con, went to the pub and didn't bother to wait for me." He turned to me. "Hello. You must be Finola. I'm Rory Quirke. Welcome to this part of the world. I hope the natives have been friendly."

"Hi, Rory." My hand disappeared in his big fist while I looked into his grey eyes and, to my annoyance, blushed. I never blush. But this man had a strange effect on me. Not film-star handsome, but nevertheless, he oozed sex appeal and self-confidence. I also knew who he was and my heart sank. One of *them*.

CHAPTER 3

"You're *that* Rory Quirke," I blurted out. "Member of the Irish parliament."

"Correct. Otherwise known as a TD," he quipped. "I wondered how long it would take you to recognise me."

"About four seconds." I eased my hand out of his grip. "I'd forgotten this was your constituency."

"Not anymore. I left politics. I didn't stand in the last election. I thought you might have heard."

"I left, too. Maybe *you* might have heard?"

"I thought you were fired."

"I resigned."

He lifted an eyebrow. "That's what they all say."

"Just like all politicians who are in danger of losing their seat say they're 'leaving'?" I said, making quote marks.

"Uh-huh." A woman laughed. "I feel a little controversy in the air. I thought Finola was here to get away from politics."

"You can never get away from politics," I replied. "Or politicians. They're everywhere."

"Not too fond of them, are you?" Rory asked.

"Depends what kind."

"Are there more than one?"

I looked at him for a moment. "There are two. The kind with a conscience and the gobshites."

"I'm afraid to ask which category you put me in."

"Good," I shot back. "Because I wouldn't tell you. But I'm not here to argue with politicians. Or criticise them."

"You're going to reveal all about us, then?" the woman asked. "We've all read your column in The Irish Telegraph. Is there going to be something similar here?"

"I'm not going to reveal my plans for the paper. But there are going to be a few surprises."

"I'm looking forward to seeing what you're going to do." the woman said. "Especially if there's going to be some hot gossip and a little dirt on the county council."

I winked. "You never know."

"Time to sit down to dinner," Miranda called from the door.

There was a contented murmur and a sudden rush through the door into a candlelit dining room. Large windows overlooked a beautiful garden, where the evening mist floated around old apple trees and shrubs.

At the big table, I found myself seated between Rory and a ruddy-faced man called Fergal, who told me he was head vet at the nearby stud farm. As he seemed more interested in his plate of couscous and Moroccan lamb stew, we didn't talk much until Rory turned to me.

"So, Finola, what are you going to do here in the sticks?" he enquired.

"I'm going to run The Knockmealdown News, as you know."

"Of course. I heard about it as soon as you got the job. News like that gets around very fast here. Any news does, as a matter of fact. You'll want to watch your step here. There are spies everywhere."

I took a swig of wine. "Spies? Really?"

"Well, you know. Twitching net curtains. Squinting windows and all that. I often wonder why we need a newspaper at all."

I laughed. "I've heard that about country towns."

He moved a little closer. "So, Finola, tell me about yourself."

"Why? I have a feeling you know everything about me already."

"Just superficial stuff. But I'd like to know more."

I tried not be affected by his eyes on me. "Like what?"

"Like why are you single? You're attractive, intelligent, funny and creative."

I managed not to blush, and fired him a sassy reply. "I'm overqualified."

He burst out laughing. "Yeah, I'd say you are. And you scare them off with all that."

"How about you? Why aren't you married?"

"Me? Oh, I'm too picky."

"Maybe it's the other way around?"

He shook his head and laughed. "Remind me never to cross swords with you."

"I will."

He sighed and picked up his wine glass. "But I think you might be right. No woman would like to be the wife of a politician."

"Must be the living death."

"Being married to me or the politician side?"

"Both. A deadly combination, I'd say." I suddenly realised the room had fallen silent. All eyes were on Rory Quirke and me. I had probably overdone the snappy answers, and now they hated me. Shit. My social skills let me down again. I went to snatch my wine glass to take a calming sip, but missed and knocked the wine all over the white lace tablecloth. Somebody gasped. Someone else tittered.

Rory came to my rescue, righting my glass and throwing his napkin over the stain. "Miranda, these lace tablecloths are very knobbly. I nearly did the same just a second ago," he called across the table.

"I know," she called back. "I'm sorry, Finola. Don't worry

about it. Easy to throw in the washing machine. I have a ton of these tablecloths in the linen cupboard, anyway. Remnants of the former occupants who were happy to leave them behind."

Jerry came around the table and filled my glass. "There you go. We can't leave you without wine."

"Thanks," I whispered to Rory. "Sorry about the hostility."

He smiled and touched my arm. "I enjoyed it. Haven't had this much fun in years." He turned to Fergal. "Did I tell you about that mare you said was in season? Well, she wasn't."

Fergal bristled beside me. "She was when I tested her. You must have just missed that window."

"Maybe," Rory said, sounding doubtful. "But whatever. Better luck next time. Not that I relish another trip with a horse box over the hill on those roads."

"Over the hill?" I asked, mystified. "What hill?"

Fergal turned to me, looking as if he had only just noticed I was there. "No hill, really, but a mountain pass. Rory was taking his mare to be covered by the stallion at the stud farm on the other side of Lismore."

"Oh," I said, mentally trying to locate Lismore on the map. "You mean Lismore with the big castle?"

He nodded. "Nice town. The castle is owned by the Duke of Devonshire. Has been for many generations. Some of the family still stay there during the summer months. I think they also come during the hunting season. You should go there. The gardens are open to visitors. A real Victorian garden. Beautiful."

"Thank you. I will. It's not that far, is it? Just over the hill."

"I'll take you there if you want. We could go next Sunday. Then we can have lunch in this great little pub. What do you say?"

I blinked. Was this ruddy-faced rugby type asking me out on a date? His eyes were kind, and there was an endearing quality about him. A gentle giant in his yellow sweater. A restful person to spend a Sunday with.

"Why not?" I replied. "That's very kind of you. Sounds interesting."

Fergal flushed and cleared his throat. "Great. I'll pick you up at around eleven. Where do you live?"

"I don't really live anywhere yet. I'm staying at the B and B near the office. A bit of a dump, but I'm sure I'll find something to rent soon."

"That B and B's run by my cousin," a woman with flaming red hair and a too-tight, orange, knitted dress cut in.

"Running it very badly," Rory said in a mocking voice. "She didn't get tourist board approval this year. Isn't that what you told me, Veronica?"

"Yes, well…" Veronica squirmed. "I suppose she should smarten it up a bit."

"That's putting it mildly," Rory muttered.

"I just had an idea," Miranda interrupted. "Why didn't I think of it before? My sister, Juliet, is letting the cottage on her farm. She was going to let it to tourists in the summer months, but you should go and have a look, Finola. She might be very happy to make a deal with you. I'll give you her phone number after dinner. It's very…quaint. "

I smiled and nodded at her. "That sounds great."

"Quaint? It's a wreck in the middle of a farmyard," Rory muttered in my ear. "Cows and horses and muck. Are you sure you could cope with that?"

I snorted a laugh. "If I can cope with the dregs of Dublin, a farmyard is no problem. Sounds charming anyway."

"Charm? It's dripping with it, girl. I bet you'll be running away screaming after a week."

"I bet you a hundred euros I won't."

He winked, spit into his hand and held it out. "Done."

After just a moment's hesitation, I spit into my own hand and shook his. It wouldn't do to look prissy.

Rory laughed and wiped his hand on his napkin. "I have feeling I'll be the loser in this one."

"You will."

"You're a gas woman, Finola McGee."

"Why, thank you." I leaned a little closer. "So here's another challenge...what the hell happened to Johnny Keegan?"

Rory stiffened. "I wouldn't go there if I were you."

"I always go down unknown paths, even when warned. They're more fun."

"You're a blow-in around here, Finola. That's a whole different kettle of fish. If you want to get on with the locals, you shouldn't shove sticks into muddy ponds. You don't know what might jump out and bite you in the butt."

"That sounds like a warning."

"Spot on."

Rory clammed up after that, and I couldn't get more than bland conversation out of him. But it didn't matter. I got what I was after. The confirmation that there was something odd about Johnny Keegan's hasty departure.

A date, a cottage, a bet, a mystery and a new challenge. Who said country life was boring?

CHAPTER 4

Miranda's sister's farm was down a boreen, more like a track than a back road, churned up by tractors, trailers and other farm machinery. I feared for my tyres as I tried to swerve around the worst potholes.

It was a beautiful spring day with blue skies. The sun shone on green fields edged with wild flowers. When I stopped briefly to take a photograph of the mountains, I could hear the lark high above my head. I craned my neck trying to spot it but could only see a quivering speck of grey and brown, too high to distinguish clearly. Amazing that such a small bird could produce such a wonderful sound. The soft breeze brought with it a smell of grass, laced with farmyard. An earthy country smell that wasn't at all unpleasant. Better than petrol fumes, anyway.

Resisting the temptation to lie down in the grass and close my eyes to the sun, I got back in the car. I had to go and look at this cottage. It would probably be a bit basic, judging by what Rory had said, but beggars can't be choosers. It had to be better than the B and B that smelled of stale bacon fat and burnt toast. I took a deep breath and stretched my back. It had been a busy day yesterday. But now, my very first issue of the paper was out there to be perused by the critical eyes of the locals. I'd made a few subtle changes. No need to make them choke on their tea and toast the very first day.

I rounded a corner and drove up what would once have been a tree-lined avenue leading through huge, rusty, iron gates flanked by ornate granite gateposts. This was more like the entrance to a country estate than a farm. There was faint lettering on one of the gateposts. I stopped briefly to try to decipher the name of the place. On closer inspection, it appeared that the name of the place was Knocknagow.

A large dilapidated country mansion came into view as I drove up a slight incline, and I pulled up in front of crumbling steps that led to a porch supported by pillars. The house would have once been beautiful and imposing, standing on a hill overlooking the winding river and the surrounding fields, dotted with cattle and sheep. I could see stables and outbuildings behind the house, so that had to be the farm part. But where was the cottage?

I climbed the steps to the front door and pulled the antiquated bell pull. There was a faint tinkling inside, but nobody came. I rang once more and then gave up, deciding to go around the back instead. As I rounded the corner, I was startled by a cacophony of barking from a collection of dogs of all sizes and breeds running towards me. A big black hound growled and showed its teeth. The others kept barking and yowling until a voice yelled "Shut up!" followed by "Down." The dogs stopped barking and the smallest one sat down.

A tall woman with short blonde hair, carrying a bundle of bandages and cotton wool came out the back door. "Yes? Are you Finola? I was hoping you'd be Fergal."

"I'm Finola," I said, wondering if I should apologise for not being Fergal. "I tried the front door, but there was no reply, so…"

She let out a raucous laugh. "That door hasn't been opened since the dawn of creation. Everyone goes around the back here." She rubbed her hand on the front of her dungarees and held it out. "Anyway, I'm Juliet, but everyone calls me Jules." Her voice was genteel, and like Miranda, she spoke with an accent that was unmistakably Anglo-Irish. But apart from the large brown eyes, you'd never have taken them for sisters.

I glanced at the dogs as I shook her hand. "Hi, Jules."

"Don't worry…they make a lot of noise but don't really attack unless they don't like you. I see that they do."

"Really?" I eyed the dogs staring back at me, not looking as if they were happy to see me. "How can you tell?"

"I just know. Listen, I'm having a bit of drama at the stables. My best hunter cut himself on a bit of wire or something, and I have to get it out. I called Fergal but only got his voicemail. Would you mind giving me a hand? I need someone to hold him while I try to stop the bleeding."

"I don't know anything about horses," I said, thinking that what didn't know about them would fill the entire Encyclopaedia Britannica.

"I'm not asking you to ride in the bloody Grand National," Jules snapped. "Come on, let's get going before he bleeds to death." She started to walk swiftly across the yard and through an archway, and I did my best to keep up with her. We raced through a second yard, where hens were strutting around, picking at the grass, and finally through a set of gates into an area lined with an L-shaped stable block. Too busy trying to follow Jules, I didn't get a chance to look around but noted a small cottage further down the path. It had to be the one that was for rent.

Jules handed me the bundle of bandages. "Hold these while I get the disinfectant in the tack room. The horse is in that loose box. Have a peep and see if he's still standing up."

I looked over the stable door. Blinded by the brilliant sunshine, it took me a moment to focus, but then I could see the outline of a big horse, snorting and shivering and rolling his eyes.

"Still standing," I called to Jules across to the door through which she had disappeared.

The Blow-In

"Good. I'll just get a head collar and the disinfectant, and then we'll get him sorted."

"Head collar?"

Jules reappeared, carrying a bottle and a leather halter. "That's what we call this," she said, holding up the halter.

"Oh."

Jules handed me the bottle. "Take this while I bring him out. Then you can hold him while I clean him up."

"Okay," I said, feeling my knees wobble. "I'll do my best."

Jules opened the stable door and went inside. I could hear her talking softly to the horse. He snorted and scraped his hooves and then limped out, led by Jules, still talking to him. He stopped and wobbled, holding up his right front leg, where blood was pouring out of a gaping wound in which a piece of wire was lodged.

"Shit, he's still bleeding. Here, hold him while I try to get the wire out."

Slightly queasy from the sight of the wound, I backed away, sweat breaking out in my armpits. This was a big horse. "I'm not sure I—"

"Fuck it, just hold him!"

I closed my eyes and grabbed the rope. The horse rolled his eyes and half reared while I dangled from the rope, my hand burning.

"Calm down," I said feebly to the horse. "Take it easy." The horse snorted and lowered himself, pulling away from me, his eyes still rolling.

"Get him to stand still, will ya," Jules grunted, making a desperate lunge for the wire.

I reached out and touched the horse's sweaty neck with a shaking hand. "Hey, horse. Calm down. We're trying to help you," I squeaked. The horse didn't seem too impressed, but stopped trying to rear and kick.

"I'm going to pull it out," Jules announced. "Hold tight."

I held onto the rope for dear life. Jules yanked the bit of

wire out of the wound. The horse let out a scream of pain but calmed down once the wire was out. He breathed and snorted for a while but stood while Jules did her best to stem the flow of blood. He screamed again and pulled back violently when she applied the disinfectant. My hand felt as if it had been burnt by hot coals, and I moaned in unison with the horse.

"What's the matter with you?" Jules grunted as she tried to wrap a bandage around the wound that was still bleeding profusely.

"My hand." I changed to the left hand and held up the right one to show how it had been stripped of skin.

Jules glanced at it. "Oh shit. Why didn't you wear gloves?"

"Um, maybe I had no idea I was going to be hanging on to a mad horse?" I suggested.

"Right, sorry. Of course you didn't. But please try to keep him steady while I try to—" She was interrupted by screeching tyres on the gravel.

Fergal jumped out of a jeep that had just pulled up. "Hang on, I'm coming," he shouted while he grabbed a bag from the front seat. "I'll put a stitch in that wound."

"About bloody time," Juliet grunted and grabbed the rope from me. "It's okay. You can let go now, Finola. Fergal will look after it."

I breathed a sigh of relief. "Thank God," I whispered and nearly sank to my knees.

It didn't take Fergal long to stitch up the wound and bandage it. He plunged a syringe into the horse's neck, massaging it when he had pulled it out. "Antibiotics," he said.

The horse, whose name was Sam, calmly allowed Fergal to finish and was then led back into his stable and given oats and hay. I could hear his contented munching as I nursed my hand.

"Cup of tea?" I heard Jules say to Fergal as he put his bag back in the jeep.

"No, got to get back to the surgery. I left an injured Labrador to come here. Glad I did. That's a nasty wound. I'll come back to give him another shot in the morning." He nodded to me. "Hi, Finola. I didn't expect you to be here playing nursemaid to a horse."

"Neither did I," I grunted. "I came to look at the cottage."

"Oh God, I completely forgot," Juliet exclaimed. "Come on, Finola, I'll put a bandage on your hand and we'll go and look at the cottage when we've had a cup of tea. Bye, Fergal. See you tomorrow," she shot over her shoulder as Fergal got into the jeep.

"Bye, Jules," he shouted over the din of the engine. "See you Sunday, Finola."

"Sunday?" Jules enquired when Fergal had driven off. "You two going on a date?"

I blew on my hand, wincing as the air hit the raw palm. "No, not really. He's just going to show me around."

"I see." Jules winked. "Just a little outing, then. But Fergal's a nice chap. You could do a lot worse."

"I'm not chasing men," I muttered while we made our way back to the house. "I'm here to do a job."

"Of course you are," Jules soothed. "I didn't mean to imply you were on the market or anything."

The dogs milled around, sniffing at our legs when we walked through the back door. We entered a lobby, where an assortment of Barbours, macs and anoraks hung from pegs under which wellies and riding boots and other assorted footwear were crammed beside an umbrella stand bristling with walking sticks, tennis rackets, riding crops and cricket bats. The place reeked of dog and wet wool. I kicked off my muddy boots and padded after Jules into a kitchen that led to a conservatory, from which there was a view of an overgrown garden and old walls.

Jules pointed to a saggy chintz sofa. "Sit down while I get something to put on that hand."

"I'm okay," I grunted, sinking down on the sofa. I jumped up again as a tiny dog yelped from the depths of the cushions. "Oh God! I seem to have sat on one of your dogs."

"That's the new puppy. Scoop him out of there."

I gingerly picked up a tiny black puppy and sat down again. The puppy found its way to my lap, where it squirmed about before it curled up and went to sleep. I didn't know quite what to do, but it seemed churlish to wake him up again. Besides, he was very cute, with his soft fur, long ears and silky tummy.

"I'm fine," I said to Jules. "No need to fuss."

"No you're not. You need Granny's salve, a bandage and a cup of tea. In that order."

Granny's salve turned out to be a cooling, soothing ointment that instantly calmed the stinging pain.

"Gosh, that's like magic," I said while Jules wound a bandage around my hand. "What's in it?"

"Nobody knows. She took the secret to her grave," Jules said with pretend gloom. "But she left enough to see us through until the next famine or world war, whichever comes first." She tied a neat bow on top of my hand. "There. Don't touch it for a couple of days. Should be fine by then."

"Thanks. Who was this granny of yours, then? Some kind of witch?"

Jules laughed. "Yes I think she must have been. A little awkward, as she was the vicar's wife."

"Really? The vicar's wife?

"That's right. She had this amazing gift of healing and telling fortunes. Everyone was scared of her. She'd have been burnt at the stake if she'd lived in the seventeenth century."

I stared at Jules. "You're having me on."

She giggled. "Yes."

"Shit, I nearly believed you."

"But there's a grain of truth in it, all the same. Granny did have special gifts. She was known for her healing powers."

"Did she live in the old vicarage?"

"Yes, she did. And so did my grandfather and my dad after him. He was the last vicar in the parish. Then the vicarage and the church were closed down, and we now have to go to Clonmel for Sunday service. But Jerry bought the house when he and Miranda were married, so she gets to live in her childhood home. We have a younger sister, Desdemona, who went to America ten years ago to work in advertising. We haven't heard from her in years."

"Desdemona?" I said. Then a lightbulb lit up in my head. "Miranda, Juliet and Desdemona. Someone in your family was a Shakespeare buff."

Jules nodded. "Yes. My father. Mother too, actually. So we're all called after women in Shakespeare's plays. Could have been worse, except Dessie got the short straw. Maybe that's why she left?"

"And you haven't heard from her in years?"

"Apart from a Christmas card every year. So we know she's still alive. She's the baby in the family. She always dreamt of going to America. So one day, she just upped and left. I expect she'll appear one day as if nothing happened and expect the fatted calf."

What a fascinating family. I was burning to know more. "What about you?" I asked. "How come you have this farm? Was it in the family?"

"Not in mine. It doesn't really belong to me. It belongs to my son, who inherited it when my husband died two years ago."

I touched her arm. "I'm sorry. Please don't feel you need to tell me anything more if you don't want to."

"I don't mind." Jules sighed and looked at her hands. "It wasn't a very happy marriage. He was a lot older than me." There was a bleak look in her eyes as she continued. "We were trying to make it work after our son was born. Ten years later, we knew it was hopeless. I was going to leave when Harry died suddenly in a hunting accident. The house and the land had already been signed over to Tony, my son. He's twelve now and finishing his first year in Clongowes. That's a Jesuit school, but they take boys of all denominations. He didn't want to go to Eton like his dad. He wants to be Irish. Quite right too, but I'm sure Harry's spinning in his grave." She sighed again. "So here I am, a thirty-two-year-old widow running a country estate for someone who'll probably end up selling it in the end. How's that for a great career?"

"But you love the place."

Jules looked back at me with sad eyes. "You're very astute. I do love it. I think I married Harry just so I could live here." She jumped up from the sofa. "But enough doom and gloom. How about that cup of tea and a scone?"

"Perfect." I stroked the warm little bundle in my lap with my finger. The puppy opened his eyes and yawned. Then he sat up and licked my hand, before he settled down again with a sigh.

"I think he's adopted you," Jules laughed when she came back from the kitchen with a tray. "Do you want him?"

"Want him?" I looked down at the puppy. Was she joking? I knew nothing about dogs, had never had one or even wanted one. Dogs and cats had never figured greatly in my life.

"Yes. You can have him if you want. Our Springer Spaniel bitch gave birth to a big litter about six weeks ago. Not sure who the father is, but I think it's the black lab down the road. A springer-spaniel-Labrador mix is not the kind of dog I can sell. But the other puppies have all found homes. I can't really cope with more dogs at the moment, so I was going to give him to Miranda, but she said her cats would go mad. Wouldn't he be nice company for you in the cottage?"

"But I haven't seen it yet."

"I know, but you'll love it. Have your tea and we'll go and have a look at it."

"Okay. But I'll make up my own mind, thank you very much," I grumbled. "I might hate it."

"You won't," Jules said in a tone that didn't allow argument.

CHAPTER 5

Jules was right. I did love it. Not quite the wreck Rory had warned me about, the cottage was nevertheless in need of some serious updating. But still, it had all the ingredients that make one fall in love with a rural retreat: glorious views of the Galtee Mountains, an apple tree in bloom in the front garden, roses rambling across the front wall, the sun shining on oak planks and a little wood-burning stove in the living room. There was also a sweet kitchen with a Belfast sink and oak cupboards, a bedroom with a wrought-iron bed and a bathroom with an old-fashioned slipper bathtub. There was a small shower cubicle, but I could see myself in that bath, looking at the view through the window.

I looked around, noting the sparse furniture and the warped sash windows that were probably horribly draughty, and wondered if I'd suddenly gone all soft in the head. This was a sharp contrast to my plush modern flat in one of the best parts of Dublin. No central heating, power shower, dishwasher, Internet connection or even a landline. What was I thinking? I'd be mad to walk into a rental agreement for such a place.

"I'll get one of the lads on the farm to give it a lick of paint," Jules said as if she could read my mind. "And I've already ordered a new mattress and two easy chairs that will go on either side of the stove. I have tons of sheets and towels you can have. And blankets and stuff. Old curtains too that are lovely but will need altering. There's a woman who does sewing. She'll run them up in no time."

"What about the Internet connection?" I asked.

"There isn't one. But you can get mobile Wi-Fi. The signal is strong here."

"No central heating?"

"No. But the stove will keep the living room nice and cosy, and there are electric radiators in the kitchen and the bedroom. I'll put in one of those wall mounted fan heaters in the bathroom for you."

"Grand," I said, my eyes drifting to the sun dipping over the mountains, then back to the cracked plaster in the ceiling.

Jules hovered in the doorway. "So?"

I laughed. "I'm probably completely bonkers, but I'll take it. And the little doggy if you'll keep him for me until I move in."

"Fabulous." Jules heaved a huge sigh and held out her hand. "Welcome to Knocknagow, Finola McGee. I think you'll be a terrific neighbour."

"I'll do my best."

"Better than the previous tenant, I'm sure."

"Who was that? Some American tourist wanting to get to know 'the real Ireland'?"

"No. Johnny Keegan. Your predecessor. And his wife and son. They loved the place."

"So why did they leave?"

Jules' eyes drifted to a spot on the wall behind me. "I don't know. They just upped and left. Maybe they wanted a change of scene?"

"Hmm," I said more to myself than anyone. "I smell a story. Or some kind of mystery."

Jules focused on me again. "Don't put your reporter's nose where it doesn't belong, Finola," she said, a cold edge in her voice. "I don't know what went on with Johnny, but a blow-in digging around in that stuff wouldn't go down well with the locals. I know, being one myself."

"Being a what? A blow-in? But your family must have been here for generations."

Jules shrugged. "It takes a while before you're considered a local around here."

"How long does it take?" I couldn't help asking.

"The same as a lawn. Three hundred years and a lot of patience."

* * *

The Saturday edition of The Knockmealdown News caused a stir in the town. Not the whole edition, but the item about me that Dan had written. Behind my back, he'd ditched the idea of ten facts and ran up a short piece. I read it in the coffee shop near my lodgings, where I nearly choked on my latte and raisin scone as I read it.

THE NAKED TRUTH ABOUT FINOLA MCGEE

By Dan O'Meara

When I heard that Finola McGee was going to be our new editor, I couldn't believe my luck. Working for this reporter, who, in a very short time became a legend in political journalism, was like a dream come true.

I'm sure most of our readers will remember how Finola and her legal-eagle friend across the pond managed to solve the murder of TD Eoin Ryan and crack the corruption case connected to a well-known software company. Not long after that, she also managed to unveil the goings-on behind a huge insurance scam that linked Boston and Dublin. Some dirty politicians are now behind bars because of her clever sleuthing. But she has assured me she has now put all that behind her and wants to enjoy the peace and quiet of the countryside and run our newspaper, making it even bigger and better than before. This is a welcome break for us here at The Knockmealdown News and our readers.

That's what we know about Finola's professional life. But what about the woman behind the legend? I've done a little research and spoken to those close to Finola during her early years and found a few facts that might surprise you. Here's Finola up close and personal:

She was the captain of both the camogie and basketball teams at school. She was known as a true-blue fighter and once even played in the basketball final with a slipped disc (her team won). She tried every sport and physical activity she came across being one of those truly driven young women we all admire (and secretly fear). Not quite ballerina material, she was kicked out of ballet school at the age of twelve but excelled at Irish dancing, in which she won several medals. Way to go, Finola!

Finola was a top student and sailed into Trinity, where she studied journalism. She got her degree in record time and then worked with the both the Labour party and Fine Gael during their various election campaigns but decided to go the journalism route. During this time, she tried her hand at abseiling, windsurfing, women's rugby and rowing.

Finola's been engaged twice, but never married. She's still looking forward to meeting Mr Right. Right, Finola? Maybe he's lurking right here in County Tipp. Not such a long way to go if it turns out to be a happy ending…we'll keep you posted!

I'm sure our readers, just like us here at the paper, are looking forward to finding out what Finola's going to do with us all. She's planning some pretty startling changes, including her own column: Finola's Country File. We're not sure what she'll be writing about, but whatever it is, you know it won't be boring!

To cap it all, there was a photo of me at the age of thirteen in an Irish-dancing costume. I was wearing braces and my smile was lopsided, making me look like a complete geek. Where on earth had he found it?

I exhaled, realising I'd held my breath while I read this horror story. Jesus, that Dan fellow had some nerve! I paid the bill and raced out of the café and down the main street, catching my breath as I reached the office building. Then rage took over, and I ran up the front steps, continued up the long stairs until I reached the office.

"Where the hell is Dan O'Meara?" I roared, making Sinead on the switchboard jump.

"He hasn't come in yet," she replied. There was a buzzing sound from the panel, and she turned her attention to the caller. "Thank you," she said. "I'll forward your message." She turned to me. "The phones have been hopping all morning. They all loved Dan's piece about you."

"Shit, it's so cringe-making, I want to die."

"No," she protested. "Not at all. I thought it was sweet and heart-warming. I loved it. It makes you a real…person."

"How fabulous."

"I can tell you're annoyed. But I love it. And it might make you less of a blow-in to people around here."

Blow-in. How I hated that word. But in a rural area, someone who wasn't Tipperary born and bred would forever be considered a stranger.

"We've nearly sold out, you know," Sinead announced. "We should really do another print run. Do you want me to call the printers and tell them?"

"No. Better to let it run out. This way we can do a bigger print run next time." I relaxed, slowly realising that Dan's piece would not only sell more copies, but also herald the new look and feel of the paper. And if it made readers feel positive towards me, that wasn't a bad thing at all. "Okay, so this was a good move by Dan. Not that I'm thrilled about having details of my love life spread all over town."

Sinead giggled. "I know. But…" She paused. "You were engaged twice? What happened?"

I hesitated, knowing anything I told her would be out on the jungle telegraph within minutes. But if I didn't say anything she might make up something worse. I sighed. "One of them fell for someone else."

"That's tough. I'm really sorry, Finola. And the other one?"

"The other one—"

"Yes?"

I shrugged. "We just weren't compatible."

Sinead looked disappointed. "I see." She was interrupted by another buzzing from the switchboard, and she turned her attention away from me.

Relieved to have been saved from explaining the real reason for my second broken engagement, I walked into my office to deal with messages and work on the next issue of the paper. I sat down at my desk and started to make a few notes as ideas began to form. I'd do a weekly column. Nothing controversial, just fun stuff about a townie getting used to the country. I'd let Dan be the main reporter, as he had the finger on the pulse of the town. I'd even let him write the little crime section I was planning. Break-ins, the odd traffic accident and whatever else he could find out from the Guarda station. Could be informative and useful. While I was busy writing, the very man strolled into my office.

I stopped mid scribble. "Hi. Where have you been? I've been waiting to give out to you about that piece."

Dan stopped in his tracks. "I tried to make you *interesting*."

"Oh, you did. Very interesting, it appears. My love life splashed all over the Saturday edition. Where on earth did you get that information? And that photo?"

"I contacted your old school and got the email address of

the girl who edited the school year book. Cathy…Hannigan. She knew all about you."

I groaned. "She would. She hated me."

"Did she? Why?"

I leant back in my chair. "She used to pick on girls who were shy and vulnerable. She had her own little clique who'd go around and intimidate anyone who didn't agree with them. But I managed to burst their little bubble and get them reported to the headmistress. Cathy Hannigan never managed to sit on me." I frowned. "God, I hate bullies."

"Who doesn't? But anyway, I'm sorry if my piece embarrassed you."

I shrugged and waved my hand at him. "Nah, it's okay. I'm happy to share my love life in public if it helps sales." I tapped my notes. "But sit down and we'll do a little brainstorming. Since it's Saturday and Sinead is manning the phones, we can go through this and then take the rest of the weekend off."

"Great. Just tell me one thing. What did you do to get kicked out of ballet school?"

I scowled at him. "I grew."

"Huh?"

"Let me put it to you this way…have you ever seen a five-foot-nine ballerina with size-seven feet?"

He laughed and shook his head. "No."

"There you go. Can we forget about it and get down to business?"

Dan sat down on the chair in front of my desk. "Of course. So—" He was interrupted by Sinead screaming in the main office.

She ran into my office, her face red. "Jesus, Mary and Joseph, do you know what I just heard?"

I stared at her. "No. Is there a fire somewhere?"

"No…no…no," she stammered. "No fire. Just Colin Foley. Coming. Here."

The Blow-In

"Colin Foley, the actor?" I stared at her, mystified. "Here?"

"Yes. To Cloughmichael," Sinead panted. "To make a movie." She drew breath and put her hand on her heart. "My friend, Kate, who works at the Bianconi Inn, just told me. They've booked the whole hotel for two months. The movie company, I mean."

"Are you serious?" I asked. "I mean, is this true?"

Sinead nodded several times. "Yes, but it's very confidential. Kate had to swear not to tell a soul until it's all official."

"So she told you immediately." Dan remarked drily. "And then you rushed in here and told us."

Sinead blushed. "Yeah, well, she is my best friend. And this is news, right?"

"Of course," I soothed. "Very exciting news. I bet every female within two hundred miles will be swooning when they hear this. But I wouldn't tell anyone else until it's official."

"Of course not," Sinead said primly. "It's *confidential*."

Dan and I looked at each other in stunned silence when Sinead had stomped out of the office.

"Colin Foley," I said. "The hottest Irishman on the planet. Here. In Cloughmichael. This is a fantastic scoop. And just after his Oscar nomination too."

"This could be great for us," Dan said. "For the town too."

"What's the movie?"

Dan shrugged. "No idea. I don't follow show business news much. Do you?"

"No, but I read Hello Magazine at the hairdresser's a few weeks ago. There was nothing else to read. The issue was a couple of months old. There was a feature about Colin, though. His marriage break-up was big news then." I didn't say I'd been so engrossed that the purple highlights had been added, as, too mesmerised by the pictures of Colin's fling with a Mexican air hostess in the Bahamas, I barely noticed what was being done to my hair.

Dan smirked. "Yeah. Saw something about that in The Sunday Times."

"What a body," I said without thinking.

Dan nodded. "She was pretty hot, yeah."

"Not her. Him," I mumbled, remembering the abs, the biceps, not to mention the rear. I shook myself and cleared my throat. "But, um, back to business. What suggestions did you have to show me?"

"It's about the website. It needs serious updating. I thought, to save money, we could get someone who's looking to start his or her own web-design business and would agree to do it for free in exchange for exposure."

"Good idea. Do you know someone like that?"

"No, but I've drawn up an ad we could put on the front page and make it stand out. In the left column, where we usually do community news. I've made up some text." Dan pushed a piece of paper across the desk. It read:

The Knockmealdown News is seeking a web designer to update our website. The position will provide invaluable skills and experience in editorial design and other aspects of the publishing environment. In addition, the successful applicant will be able to showcase his/her talents in web design and setting up websites for their own design business. Applicants must be proficient in Adobe CS, in particular InDesign and Photoshop, and have an interest in editorial design. Please send your CV along with samples of design work to Dan O'Meara, at the Knockmealdown News head office, Cloughmichael.

"I'll set up a Facebook page and Twitter account for us too."

I stared at him. "You mean we don't have those?"

"No. Johnny never did that social media stuff. He was kind of busy with—" Dan stopped. "Other problems," he ended.

"What problems?"

Dan shrugged. "Not for me to say. But once I set those things up, we can mention this there too."

Wondering what 'problems' Johnny Keegan had been dealing with, I pushed the paper back at Dan. "Excellent. Get Mary to run that in the Thursday edition."

"Okay." He got up. "Do you want to break the news about the movie in that issue?"

"I think we must. We might just get it in before it's all over the country. Tell Sinead to keep her mouth shut, and make sure she tells her friends to do the same."

"Hmm, I doubt we'll be able to stop them. But I'll do my best."

The phone rang. It was Jules. "Hi, Finola," she whispered. "Sorry to disturb you at the office, but I have something to tell you..."

"What is it? Why are you whispering?"

"All very hush-hush, but you should know that an American company called Mira—something, have contacted me about a film they're going to make right here in Cloughmichael."

"Miramax?"

"That's it. They want to use the house as one of their sets. And the stables. They'll be setting up all the trailers and movie equipment on the front lawn."

"Really?" I said, deciding to hear her end of the story before I said anything. "What's the movie about?"

"A story set just before the nineteen sixteen rising. Some romantic crap about a young girl from an aristocratic family falling in love with an Irish rebel. Complete rubbish, I'm sure. The movie will be something like the Titanic story. And some big star will be playing the main part. I don't go to the cinema much and I don't watch TV, so I've no idea who he is. The set will be closed to all outsiders, so you'll have to have some kind of badge to go in and out. I wouldn't have agreed if it wasn't for the money they offered for the use of the house and grounds. And they want to use the horses too. It'll all help pay for some urgent repairs. As I said, very hush-hush, but I thought I'd tell you, as the place is going to be quite noisy during the next few months. I hope you don't mind. If you want to pull out of renting the cottage, I quite understand."

"Not at all. I'm sure I can cope," I said, trying to keep the glee out of my voice. I couldn't believe my luck. I'd be up close and personal to the cast and crew. We could run this as a serial in the paper once it got rolling. And as no other media would have access to the set, The Knockmealdown News would have the exclusive…if I could swing it with the movie company. My mood plunged. That probably wouldn't work. They were too big for us. But living on the set, as it were, I might have been able to weasel my way in some way. I'd faced bigger challenges like this in my chequered past.

Jules' voice cut into my musings. "Not a word to anyone about this."

"Of course not," I lied. "When are they coming?"

"The director and producer have already been here to look at locations. But the cast and crew aren't coming until the beginning of June."

"I see." The beginning of June. Only a couple of weeks away. No time to waste. I had to plan what I was going to do with this. Maybe write a clever little teaser or something.

"They're looking for extras too. So they'll be announcing that soon," Jules continued. "Might be something fun for the locals."

I blinked. There it was. The little opening I'd been looking for. "Brilliant! I'll look into that. We could run the ad for them. Must go. Thanks for calling, Jules. I'll see you during the week to plan for my move into the cottage." I hung up and stuck my head out the door yelling for Dan. What Jules just said had given me the idea I was looking for. The next issue of the paper would soon have the town talking. And increase our circulation a little bit.

I felt the buzz of a new start and a whole new life for this little country newspaper.

Chapter 6

Coming back from a run on Sunday morning, I came to a halt in front of the B and B, wiping my face and pulling my sweaty tee shirt away from my skin. It was the first time in months I'd been out for a run. My fitness level was down to zero, which came as no surprise. I bent over, put my hands on my knees and tried to get my breathing back to normal. While I was recovering, I noticed someone getting out of a car that had just pulled up. Someone faintly familiar. Someone all washed and brushed and dressed in country tweeds. Shit. Fergal. I'd forgotten we had a date.

"Hi, Finola," he said as he approached. "I hope I'm not late?"

"No," I panted. "You're early."

He looked at his watch. "It's five past eleven."

I straightened up, wishing I had a towel to wipe my dripping face. "I'm sorry, Fergal, but I completely forgot about our date."

His face fell. "Oh. So what do you want me to do? Will we reschedule? I can come back another Sunday. It's my only day off, so—"

I suddenly felt as if I'd kicked a puppy. "No, it's okay. I'll just have a quick shower, if you don't mind waiting for a few minutes?"

He brightened. "Of course not. I'll wait in the car. Need to check my messages anyway."

"Great. I won't be long." I raced through the door and into my room and jumped into the shower, thankful my hair was short and would dry in no time. I quickly showered, dried myself and got dressed. Jeans, light-blue shirt and a grey sweater seemed appropriate for a sightseeing-with-lunch kind of date. A dash of blusher and mascara, and I was good to go. My hair still damp, I ran out the door and arrived at the car, breathless.

Fergal looked up from his phone. "That was quick." He glanced at his watch. "Ten minutes. Must be some kind of record for a woman."

"I'm not a woman, I'm me. Put that phone away and let's go."

He laughed and did what he was told.

I opened the passenger door and transferred a bag full of syringes, a dog lead and a halter to the back seat. "I suppose this is your travelling surgery."

Fergal started the engine. "Sorry about that. I had a couple of calls before I came here. I normally use my jeep for work, but the car's handier sometimes. Don't worry, a friend's covering for me today, unless there's a big drama somewhere."

"Like what?"

He shrugged. "You never know with horses, especially thoroughbreds. They're very fragile. And extremely valuable…as you probably know."

"Sort of," I said as my eyes drifted to the beautiful landscape rolling by.

We drove out of town and down country roads towards the mountains rising up before us. I was about to break the silence, when Fergal took a sharp turn and drove past the gates of an old house and up a narrow twisting lane, on either side of which a carpet of purple flowers stretched as far as I could see. I was speechless. It was like entering some kind of paradise, silent and sheltered from the wind.

"Oh," I whispered. "My God, what *is* this?

"Rhododendrons." Fergal pulled up. "Let's stop here for a while."

"Oh yes," I sighed. "This is incredible. I've never seen anything like it."

Fergal nodded. "It's pretty stunning all right. But it's not all so wonderful. The rhododendrons have spread like wildfire in this area. They thrive in this acid soil, and they're creating problems for the environment because of their nasty habit of taking over and causing native plants to die out."

I kept looking at the wonderful vista. "It's not a native plant?"

"No, it was brought here in the nineteenth century from India by landowners who wanted exotic plants for their gardens. Then they thrived in our mild climate and fertile soil and went completely mad."

"I can see that," I remarked and picked up my phone. I opened the window and took a shot of the purple valley and the white butterflies flitting from bloom to bloom. "It's kind of surreal, like something from a movie."

Fergal started the car. "Very true. Beautiful, but with a nasty undertone."

We drove on, up a steep road full of hairpin bends, through pine woods and heather. The views of the valley and the Galtee Mountains beyond were breathtaking. We stopped briefly at the mountain pass called the Vee and looked at the lake, dark and brooding between the mountains. What a magic, mystical landscape this was.

I turned to Fergal. "Thank you for taking me on this trip. I never knew this county was this interesting and beautiful. It's a shame Dubliners know so little about these rural areas."

"Yes it is. But maybe you should spread the word? Write about it."

I nodded. "Yes. Good idea. I was planning to have my own blog, anyway. I wasn't quite sure what I'd write about, though. But now I do."

"I look forward to reading it. Let's get going. It's about another half hour to Lismore. We'll have time for a little sightseeing before lunch."

The landscape was different on the other side of the mountain pass. We drove through green fields, then down the hill into dense, leafy woods with lush vegetation. I spotted palm trees and ferns, feeling as if we were in a subtropical forest.

"It's more sheltered here," Fergal explained. "We're near the castle, and this is part of the property and gardens. They brought in all these exotic plants many years ago, and now it's gone a bit wild."

"It's like a jungle. I wouldn't be surprised to see a parrot. Or monkeys swinging from the vines."

Fergal laughed. "I know what you mean." He glanced at me and touched my hand. "Are you enjoying the drive?"

"Very much," I replied, wondering how I could get this silent man to say more than one sentence at a time. Good-looking in a horsey way, he was solid, dependable and—boring. But he'd taken me on a lovely tour of the back country and shown me parts of Tipperary I didn't even know existed. A good man with a true-blue heart. A very rare species these days.

We arrived at the edge of Lismore village, where the towers of a fairy-tale castle rose above the river and the old bridge. After parking in the main street lined with quaint old houses, we visited the medieval church and its ancient graveyard, where many of the gravestones bore inscriptions from as far back as the sixteenth century. The sun warmed our backs as we walked around, reading the names and imagining how the people had lived and died.

"So many women dying young," I remarked, reading the faint letters on a headstone. "This one was only twenty-two."

"Childbirth," Fergal said. "They often married at sixteen or so, had a couple of children and then died. The children often died, too. Tough times for women."

"Very tough." Suddenly chilled despite the hot sun, I wrapped my arms around myself. "For anyone."

Fergal put his hand on my shoulder. "Yes. Pestilence, war and bad living conditions. Nobody lived very long. The vibes of all that are still around. Can you feel them?"

I leaned against him, oddly comforted by his gesture. "Yes. I think I can." I shivered.

Fergal gave my shoulder a little squeeze before he let it go. "Let's have lunch."

"Good idea."

Over beer, quiche and salad in a cosy pub near the castle, I tried to prod Fergal about the people in the town, especially Johnny Keegan.

Unlike everyone else I had asked, Fergal didn't mind telling me what he knew. "Ah, good old Johnny," he said. "Lovely man. We used to go fishing together."

"So why did he leave?"

Fergal frowned. "I don't know the whole story, but I think it had something to do with his wife and her son. He married a woman from Croatia about three years ago. She had a son who was about ten when they got married. They didn't quite fit in here. I think she found it hard to make friends. And the boy had serious problems at school. I think the other kids were mean to him. But I was so busy at the stud during the six months before they left. January's foaling season and then the sales at Goffs…"

"So you lost touch?"

Fergal took a swig of his beer. "Yes. And when I got back to him, they were already packing up to leave. Something weird going on there, I thought."

"But you never found out what it was?"

"No. But I had the impression Johnny was angry, and…" Fergal hesitated.

"And?"

"Scared."

"Scared? Why do you say that?"

Fergal was about to speak when were interrupted by someone standing at our table. I looked up. It was Rory Quirke.

He touched Fergal's shoulder. "Hi there. Thought I'd find you here."

"How did you know I'd be here?" Fergal asked.

"My dog got sick. I rang your surgery, but I was told you were off today, and that useless eejit you call assistant said he was on duty. But I remembered you asked Finola to come on an outing here, so I went to find you. Then I saw your car parked outside and used my tiny brain…" He paused for a moment. "Hi, Finola."

I nodded trying to stay as cool as he looked. "Hi there, Rory." I smiled, taking in his tall frame dressed in jeans and scuffed suede jacket over a tight tee shirt. His face was strained, and there was something close to panic in his eyes.

"What's up with the dog?" Fergal asked.

"Poison," Rory said. "We were out walking in the hills and she ate something—a rat or a fox that had been poisoned. She got sick about an hour afterwards, and now she's nearly paralysed."

Fergal got up. "Where is she?"

"In my jeep parked outside. It's Nellie, my Irish setter."

"Nellie? Jaysus." Without another word, Fergal ran out of the pub, Rory at his heels.

I paid the bill and followed them into the street, where I found the two men carrying the dog to Fergal's car.

Fergal turned to me when they had laid the unconscious dog on the back seat. "I'm going to take her straight to the surgery. My car's more comfortable and faster than Rory's. Finola, you go with Rory, and I'll catch up with you as soon as I've dealt with this. Rory, please call my assistant and tell him what happened, and ask him to set up the equipment.

Just say it's a poisoned Irish setter. He'll know what I'll need."

Rory nodded. "Grand."

After ensuring the dog was comfortable, Fergal drove off, leaving Rory and me standing there, staring at each other in an awkward silence.

Rory took a car key from his pocket and opened the door of his battered Land Rover. "Get in so. Sorry about the mess. Didn't know I'd be driving a lady."

"I'm no lady." I shoved assorted farm paraphernalia from the passenger seat and climbed in.

"I know. I was being sarcastic." He climbed in beside me and started the engine, and we drove in silence away from the village and up the road Fergus and I had driven along earlier.

Rory's face was white, and his jaw clenched as we went up the steep hill to the Vee.

"I'm so sorry about your dog," I said as gently as I could. "You must be worried."

Rory nodded. "Yeah. I love that bitch. But I don't suppose you'd understand if you don't have a dog."

"I do." My thoughts went to the little black puppy, and I felt a pang of love. He was already mine in my heart.

He glanced at me with surprise. "You have a dog? Here?"

"At Jules's. She's minding him until I move into the cottage. A puppy that kind of wormed his way into my heart. Sounds silly, doesn't it?"

"Not a bit. Dogs have habit of stealing your heart."

"They certainly do."

We were quiet again all the way across the Vee, down the steep road and the spectacular view, through the magic valley with the rhododendrons.

"Pretty," Rory said. "But destructive."

"I know."

"Sorry. Not feeling very chatty right now."

"Of course not. Is Fergal's clinic far?"

"Just outside town, but if we take a shortcut, we'll catch up with him."

I pulled my phone from my bag. "Do you want me to call him?"

"Good idea," Rory grunted.

I found Fergal's number in my contact list, pressed call and turned the speaker on.

He replied on the first ring. "Finola? We got here about fifteen minutes ago. Tell Rory Nellie's having her stomach pumped, and we're trying to find an antidote. She's on a drip and seems a little more comfortable. No need to come in yet. We'll call him when we have any further news."

"Got that," Rory shouted across me. "We'll wait in the pub across the street. Give us a shout when you have any news."

"Will do," Fergal promised. "Sorry about our date, Finola, but I'll make it up to you another time."

"That's okay," I told him. "I really enjoyed the drive and the lunch. Thank you, Fergal. See ya."

"Very considerate of you, as you paid for lunch," Rory remarked after I'd hung up.

I shrugged. "That's okay. It wasn't the kind of date where the man pays, anyway. I assumed we'd share the bill, but then Fergal got busy. He can pay next time."

Rory pulled up outside a thatched cottage which sported a sign saying 'The Thatched Roof' over its red half-door. "Next time? Is there going to be a next time?"

"Who knows?"

He peered at me. "You got on well, then?"

I gave him a cool stare. "Like a house on fire."

He burst out laughing. "I can imagine. I bet you did most of the talking. Listen, how about a pint while we wait? Fergal's clinic is just opposite. I need something after that scare, and it would be nice to have some company."

"Why not? A pint sounds nice." I met his twinkling eyes, and I suddenly felt the day had improved by at least a hundred percent. The boring date had turned into something quite different.

CHAPTER 7

We walked into the dimly lit pub and sat down at a table near the roaring turf fire, welcome after the chill of the spring evening. The place was slowly filling up with people who had been at the Gaelic football match at the GAA grounds nearby. There was a cheerful atmosphere, and many people came up and shook hands with Rory. One of them, a fit-looking man with a boyish face and curly brown hair, grabbed my hand.

"Hi there, Finola. Welcome to our little town. I'm Oliver O'Keefe. TD."

"Rory's replacement?" I said, pulling my hand out of the bone-crushing handshake.

"I wouldn't say that," he replied, the smile stiffening. "I won on my own ticket."

"Of course," I said. "I didn't mean to imply anything else." I'd heard about him and his popularity in Cloughmichael, and I wasn't surprised. This man oozed charm and charisma that would impress the average voter. Except I didn't buy it. There was something false and self-serving about this man.

"Thanks for the welcome," I said to cover up my slight dislike.

He touched my shoulder. "Very happy you've come to rescue the dear old Knockmealdown News. It deserves to keep going. I'm sure you'll lift it from the doldrums and make it shine again."

"I'll do my best."

Oliver nodded at Rory. "Great to see you, Rory," he said before he walked away.

Rory smiled at me apologetically once we had two brimming pints in front of us. "Sorry about that."

"That's okay. You're well known around here, I see."

"Yes. I've been representing this town for the past five years. But now Oliver has taken over my seat. He'll do a great job." He raised his glass. "Cheers, Finola."

I raised my own pint. "Cheers, Rory. I hope your dog will be okay."

"I'm sure she will. I got Fergal in time. He's a superb vet, you know."

"Yes. I've seen him in action. I watched him stitch up Jules's horse the other day. Seems very skilled."

"That's for sure." Rory put down his glass. "But enough about him. I read the piece about you. Interesting. You were one busy girl. Ballet, Irish dancing, gymnastics. And that was only on Thursdays, I bet."

I laughed and wiped the foam off my lip. "Yeah, I think I must have been hyperactive."

"Or you were running away from home?"

I squirmed. He'd hit a nerve. I was involved with a million after-school activities in my teens. Not only because I loved being physically active but also because that way, I could avoid going home in the early evening and have to listen to my dad's bad-tempered rants. Home was not a happy place for a teenage girl.

"So tell me about this town," I said to change the subject. "I've only been here a short time, but I have noticed a few things that puzzle me."

"Such as?"

"The main street is full of empty shops. Why?"

Rory sighed. "One of my pet hates. You want me to get on my hobby horse?"

"If you can explain the problem, yes."

Rory took another swig of his pint. Then he put his glass down and leant forward. "It's to do with the fucking county council and their money-grabbing stupidity," he said with such venom, I jumped. He started counting on his fingers. "One, the rents of the shops are too high. Two, the rates are also very high, and three, they insist on charging for parking, which is ridiculous in such a small town. All that has contributed to these small businesses having to close down. We used to have some really nice shops in the main street—a hardware store, a jeweller's, a bookshop, a bakery and an antique shop. All gone because of what I've just said. I've tried to air these issues to the county councillors, but nobody will listen."

"Is that why you left politics?" I asked.

"Yes. Partly. Lots of other things too, which I can't go into right now."

"Has it got anything to do with Johnny Keegan and why he left?"

Rory nodded, a bitter line around his mouth. "In a way." He paused while he looked at me intently. "You're a reporter, Finola. You always tell the truth and get to the root of every problem. Maybe you can raise these issues in The Knockmealdown News?"

I fiddled with my glass. "I'm not sure." I looked back at him, trying to see the answer in those honest grey eyes. "I was a reporter, Rory. But I was totally burnt out by the last corruption scandal. I wanted to leave all that and do something less…less controversial. I needed a break. That kind of thing is very stressful, you know. I've put my career on the line many times. I don't know if I want to do that anymore. The quiet life is looking increasingly attractive."

He nodded. "I see. I didn't take you for a quitter. No more standing up for what's right, then."

Angered by the disdain in his eyes, I got up. "You've quit,

too, Rory Quirke. If you really wanted to fight, you'd have stayed in politics. But now you want other people to fight your battles."

"That's not what I meant."

"That's what it looks like from here. And in my case, I have other people to consider. The paper's in trouble. Jerry and Miranda need me to turn things around. I want to update the whole look and introduce new features. I want to make it commercial, to use a dirty word in journalism. Yes…cheesy, cute, attractive to people around here. A fun read, something to brighten their week. I'm done with the dirty digging. You never win, anyway. That's the real deal."

He didn't reply. We stared at each other for a moment in a silent battle. I dug into my pocket and threw a five-euro note on the table. "That should cover the cost of the pint. I hope your dog will be okay. I'll walk back to the B and B. Goodbye." Then I marched out of the pub, my head held high. And my heart in my shoes.

* * *

I called him Jake. I don't know why the name seemed to suit him, but he reacted to it straightaway. Strange how a small puppy can walk straight into your heart, but that's exactly what Jake did, that first day at Jules's. Leaving him behind was a huge wrench. I could still feel his warm little body in my lap every time I drove back to town and the B and B that now felt even more soulless and lonely. The two weeks of refurbishing and updating the cottage dragged into three weeks as small problems with plumbing and wiring cropped up. I busied myself with the paper and the modernisations I wanted to introduce.

It was going well. We saw a small but steady increase in circulation with every passing week. The website was also coming along, with the new website designer, an Italian woman working from Cork who was setting up her web-design business and needed exposure. We also got a few new sponsors both for the paper and the website: small local businesses that were happy to advertise with us. But I needed to get more important sponsors, big names in cosmetics, cars, computers and whatever else was trending out there. An exclusive about the movie that would be shot in the town would help a lot to attract these big names. Not likely, but as I'd be living next door to the main set, I could at least do a special with a personal slant.

I didn't realise then quite how personal it would be.

* * *

I moved into the cottage the following Sunday, the day before the film crew was due to arrive. There wasn't much to move, except my two suitcases, my laptop and a box of books, none of which were difficult to handle. Jules had furnished the cottage with items from the big house she didn't need, and I added to that with a new bedspread for the wrought-iron bed, a mahogany chest of drawers and a leather armchair from a second-hand furniture shop in nearby Clonmel. Jules lent me a beautiful Indian rug from one of her guest rooms for my new living room and a sheepskin for the floor of my bedroom.

I put Jake's old cushion from Jules's in front of the stove in the living room, but he ignored it and jumped onto my bed as soon as I'd made it and made himself comfortable on the new white bedspread. I didn't chase him away. It would have been nice to have company in bed, even if this was the only kind of male I was likely to cuddle up to.

Having gone to sleep enjoying the silence, I woke up at the crack of dawn by a cacophony of noise. A cock screamed in my ear, adding to the dawn chorus of what sounded like a million birds. I groaned and looked at my watch. Five o'clock. Shit.

"I thought the country would be quiet," I said to Jake, who opened one eye, wagged his tail, snuggled up to my feet and went back to sleep.

My eyes heavy, I managed to drift off, only to be woken up again by the still-excited cock and a tractor trundling up the lane behind the stables. Groggy with sleep, I dragged myself out of bed. It was six o'clock, too early for anything except a cup of tea. I threw on my fleece dressing gown, stuck my feet into my furry slippers and made my way to the kitchen, where the sun streamed in through the sash windows, making pools of light on the flagstones. The kitchen was freezing, so I turned on the electric heater, made myself a cup of tea and took it to the little patio in the front garden. I sat down on the garden seat and enjoyed the warmth of the sun, my cup of tea and the birds singing their little hearts out. Jake padded out to join me. He sat down by my feet and yawned.

"I know," I said. "It's too early to be up. But isn't it pretty?" I added, looking out at the garden with the apple tree in full bloom, the roses just unfurling their buds and further away, the mountains, their slopes like a patchwork quilt of green, brown, yellow and purple. A heavenly view, even if I needed sleep. I made a mental note to myself to buy industrial-strength ear plugs and blackout curtains. I was about to go back inside when something weird happened.

Slurping the last drops of tea from the mug, I noticed a movement in the shadows of the big laurel bush by the gate. Jake jumped up and started to bark. The figure of a man came into view. He was dressed in jeans, a dark-green sweater and walking boots. Not just any man, I realised with shock as he smiled at me. I knew that face, those green eyes and floppy blond hair, not to mention that body. Colin Foley, the heart-throb of the century was standing by my fence smiling at me. I blinked, clutching at my half-open dressing gown, the mug slipping from my hand onto the tiles. This had to be some kind of dream.

"Hi," he said. "I'm sorry if I disturbed you."

"No problem," I croaked, running my hand through my hair in a futile attempt to look a little less wrecked. "Lovely morning, isn't it?"

"Fabulous. Cute house."

I picked up the mug. "Thank you."

Without asking for permission, he opened the gate and strolled up the path, holding out his hand. "I'm Colin Foley."

Still clutching my dressing gown, I shook his hand. "Hi, Colin, I'm Finola. Finola McGee."

"Nice to meet you."

"Nice to meet *you*," I stammered. "Shut up, Jake."

Jake stopped barking and we stared at each other for a while. Well, I stared while Colin bent over to pat Jake. Up close, he looked a little less Colin Foley the megastar than in the media or on screen. Older, tired, unshaven, a hint of bags under those famous eyes, bloodshot from either a lack of sleep or too many beers, I couldn't quite decide which. Still gorgeous but more human and a lot more normal than in the glossy publicity shots.

He straightened up and noticed me staring. "You okay?"

"Yes. Fine. It's just, um, a little strange to find you here at this hour."

He laughed. "Yeah, I suppose. I shouldn't even be here. But I arrived yesterday and got to the hotel very late. Then I couldn't sleep. Jetlag or something. So I decided to come and see the set and wander around just to get the feel of the place. And then I saw your cottage and wanted to take a closer look. I didn't mean to disturb you."

"That's all right. I'm already disturbed. I mean, I was already up because of the racket."

"What racket?"

"The cock crowing at five in the morning, the birds chirping and twittering. And I thought the countryside would be quiet."

"Not a country girl, then?"

"Definitively not. I'm Dublin born and bred."

He laughed and nodded. "Yeah. Me too. What part?"

"Glasnevin. You?"

"Inchicore. Working class then, trendy as hell now." His LA twang became more Dublin-speak. He peered at me. "Your name rings a bell. I've been out of the country for a long time, based in LA mostly. But I have a feeling I've seen your name in the media somewhere." He paused, his brow furrowed in thought. Then he brightened. "Finola McGee, the reporter, right? The one who cracked that murder-and-corruption case in Boston. That's you, isn't it?"

I held up a hand, forgetting to hold on to my dressing gown. "Guilty."

"Wow."

I closed my dressing gown, realising he must have caught a glimpse of my flimsy nightie. "Sorry."

He looked confused. "About what? Being you?"

"No. About flashing my boobs at you."

He flicked his hand at me. "Oh, that. Nice, but I get that all the time. Great boobs, though."

"Thank you." I suddenly giggled at the ridiculousness of the situation.

Colin shot me one of his trademark thousand-watt smiles. "You're just like I imagined."

I stared at him. "You imagined me? Jesus, that's—I don't know what it is. Incredible."

He laughed. "Have you…er…imagined me?"

"I didn't have to. You're everywhere. TV, magazines, newspapers, you name it, you're out there."

"Yeah, I know. No mystery there. Except they're all lying."

He pulled out the garden chair beside mine. "Mind if I sit down? The jetlag is suddenly getting to me."

"Please, sit down. Would you like a cup of tea?"

He sank down on the chair, squinting against the sun. "Only if it's Barry's."

"Need you ask? I only ever drink Barry's tea. I could even stretch to a slice of soda bread with some Old Time Irish marmalade."

"Heaven."

While the kettle boiled, I rushed into the bedroom and pulled on a pair of jeans, a tee shirt and my Aran fisherman's sweater, quickly brushing my hair and splashing cold water on my face. Then I made a fresh pot of tea and spread butter and marmalade on a couple of slices of soda bread and carried a tray with this feast out to the patio. Colin had scooped a happy Jake onto his lap and was busy cooing at him. Jake licked Colin's face and jumped down to meet me.

I put the tray on the table. "Here you go. Not a full Irish, but all I have to offer at the moment."

He grinned. "I wouldn't say that."

I rolled my eyes. "How cheesy."

"Sorry. I can't help it. It's like some kind of tic."

I poured him a mug of tea and splashed some milk into it. "Sugar?"

"No just milk." He grabbed a slice of bread and took a big bite. "This tastes like home. And you. You're so…so Irish." He sighed wistfully. "God, I've missed this country." As the sun rose higher, he slipped on a pair of sunglasses he'd fished out from his shirt pocket.

"Why don't you move back, then?" I couldn't help asking.

"Can't."

"Why?"

"Money. Tax. Work. Career."

"Oh."

He slid the sunglasses down his nose and peered at me.

"But what is Finola McGee doing here in the sticks? Writing another book?"

"No. I just got fed up with the rat race. I didn't have the energy to wrestle with corruption anymore."

"That's understandable. You fought the good fight." He pushed his sunglasses back up. "I know how you must have felt. Dirty business. Ireland sure isn't the Ireland I left. Dublin isn't my town anymore. You know what I mean?"

"Of course. That's why I'm here."

He kept looking at me. "The good old values no longer exist."

"Not that they were there in the first place," I retorted. "But way back, it was more honest. In a crooked way, if you see what I mean."

"I do. The dirty old town is no more, is it? Now it's slick and modern and…filthy underneath." He sounded sad.

I nodded. "Yeah."

He swallowed the last of the bread, slurped some tea and got up. "Got to go. My publicist is arriving this morning and the rest of the production team. Meetings, rehearsals, the whole ballet. But…" He paused, looking suddenly shy. "I'd like to see you again, Finola. I liked talking to you."

"Me too."

"Let me have your phone number. I'll give you a call."

"Okay." I went inside and found a piece of paper and scribbled my number on it and handed it to Colin.

He put it in his pocket. "Thanks for the tea and sympathy. And for the delicious breakfast."

"You're welcome. Bye, Colin."

"Bye. See you soon, I hope, Finola."

"Me too," I whispered, as I watched him saunter away.

CHAPTER 8

I stared at the computer screen and tried to concentrate on the list of applicants for the trainee journalist post we'd advertised in all the national newspapers. We needed another reporter, and I thought someone fresh from university would make a good addition to our staff. And we wouldn't have to pay much of a salary. Miranda and Jerry had promised to clean up their guest room for any out-of-town recruit. But my mind kept wandering to my early morning adventure. Colin Foley sitting on my little patio in the early morning sun. He was nothing like the image he projected in the press. His Dublin roots made him especially endearing to me. We spoke the same language, shared the same childhood memories. A kindred spirit of sorts.

The phone rang. It was Rory. "Just to tell you Nellie is all right. And…"

"Yes?"

"Sorry about the aggro last week. I didn't mean to criticise you and your work."

"Maybe I should apologise?" I offered. "I mean I was the one who stomped out of the pub in a huff."

"But you were provoked. I'd have punched me in the face."

I couldn't help laughing. "Yeah, that popped into my mind. But I didn't think being arrested for assault would add to my image as a blow-in."

"Let's forget about it." He cleared his throat. "I was thinking that… well, that I'd like to see you again. I'd like to show you my farm."

"I'd love to see it."

"Do you ride?"

"Never been on a horse in my life. Except if a donkey ride at the age of six on the pier in Bray counts."

"Afraid not. But I have a nice old nag you could sit on. He's so quiet, he's nearly asleep. I'd put my granny on him. Completely bombproof."

"Um…well…" I didn't know what to say. Me on a horse? That was something I'd never contemplated.

"Or are you too chicken?" Rory laughed.

The word chicken always got to me. It didn't fail this time. "Of course not," I chortled. "Sounds like fun. When is this event going to take place?"

"How about this evening? The weather's lovely, and it won't get dark until around nine."

"Why not? Just tell me where the farm is and I'll be there around six, when I've finished at the paper. What do I wear for riding?"

"Jeans, boots and a smile. I'll email you the directions."

I thanked him and hung up. Then I turned my attention back to the computer screen. I was reading up on the first candidate when Dan burst into my office. I looked up. "Do come in, Dan."

He squirmed. "Oh, yeah. Sorry. Should have knocked."

"Never mind. Where's the fire?"

"No fire. I just thought I'd tell you I've looked up all the applicants, and there's only one I'd hire. The rest are useless. They can't write to save their lives."

"So which one is it?"

"A woman called Audrey Killian. She's from around here. Somewhere near Dundrum, but she's been studying journalism in Dublin for the past four years and has written a few articles for The Leinster Leader that I thought were terrific. She has a short, snappy style and a great sense of humour." Dan drew breath.

I scrolled down the list and opened her application. "Looks good. She's just finished her masters. And if you like how she writes, it's okay with me. Could you email her and tell her she's got the job?"

Dan's eyes lit up. "Fantastic. I'll do that straight away. Anything else?"

"Yes. You can tell me how on earth I'm going stay on a horse for more than a second."

"What? You're going riding?"

"Yes. I've been invited to look around Rory Quirke's farm on horseback. Would be lovely if I had a clue how to ride."

Dan laughed. "Ah, sure you'll be grand, Finola. You're very fit, and I'm sure Rory has something quiet for you to ride."

"So he said." I got up. "Could you make sure everyone's on track with whatever they had to finish today and lock up? If I'm still alive tomorrow, I'll get going on my weekly column. I have to get into whatever you wear when you fall off a horse."

"Good luck," Dan called after me.

"Thanks. I'll need it," I called over my shoulder as I left, still wondering what the hell I was getting into.

I consulted Jules. "Tell me I'm crazy, but tonight I'm going riding for the first time in my life," I said as I walked in on her feeding the dogs.

Jules looked up from filling bowls with dog food. "Riding? Where?"

"At Rory Quirke's place." I held up a hand. "Not a date so don't get any ideas."

Jules smirked. "Another not-a-date date?"

"Shut up. It's not."

"And you wouldn't be the slightest bit attracted to Rory Quirke?"

"Not the slightest," I said, willing my cheeks not to flush.

Jules put the bowls on the floor and the dogs rushed into the utility room and started to munch and slurp. She straightened up and wiped her hands. "Let's have a cup of tea, if you have time?"

"Yes. It's only half past four. I said I'd be at Rory's at six. It's not far from here, is it?"

"No. Only up the road and halfway down the hill after that. By the way, what's your shoe size?" she asked over her shoulder.

"Seven. Why?"

"Oh, big. But I think I have a pair of proper riding boots that size in the boot room. And a helmet."

I followed her into the kitchen. "Brilliant. That'll make it easier."

Jules switched on the kettle. "The riding, yes. Handling the mammy will be a different matter."

"The mammy?" I said, mystified.

Jules turned to face me. "Rory's mother is the classic cliché of the Irish mammy. Domineering, possessive and a control freak. Sadly, Rory doesn't see it, but she's ruled his life since he was born. No woman has measured up to what she thinks her darling boy deserves. In fact, I think she doesn't want him to get married at all. He's been in and out of relationships for years, and I suspect he had a girlfriend in Dublin when he was in politics. I've no idea if he's still seeing her. He never brought her here. Too scared of what Mammy would say."

My mouth hung open. "What? I don't believe you. Rory seems so together and really grounded. Sure of himself and what he wants. He was a TD, for God's sake. You can't survive in politics if you're a mammy's boy."

Jules shrugged and put two mugs of tea on the table. "I'm only telling you what's common knowledge around here. Of course, Breda Quirke looks like a perfectly nice woman when you meet her casually."

"But she's really the mammy from hell?"
"If you get involved with her son, yes."
"I'll do my best not to, then."
"Good luck with that," Jules muttered.

* * *

I didn't get to meet Breda Quirke, the mammy from hell, straight away. I had to go through the baptism of fire called riding a horse first. I drove the short distance to Rory's farm with Jake in the front seat. He had looked so sad when I prepared to leave, so I allowed him to jump into the car and come with me. Why have a dog and then leave him home alone all the time?

The farm was in the middle of the rolling hills I could see from my little front garden. It was a beautiful place, with cattle and horses grazing in green fields and a big white farmhouse in the middle. I parked in front of the porch, and Rory came out as soon as I turned off the engine.

"Hi there." He eyed my boots. "I'm glad you got yourself kitted out properly."

"Jules lent me a pair of hers. And a helmet."

"Perfect. Let's go to the stables. The horses are already tacked up."

"Tacked up?"

Rory smiled. "Yes. That's what we say when we mean saddled and bridled."

"Okay. I already know a halter is really called a head collar. So I'll add that to the list of horsey terms I need to learn."

"There isn't that much to it."

"That's easy for you to say. But lead on…let's get this over with."

"Come this way, and I'll introduce you to Charlie. That's the horse you'll be riding."

With Jake at our heels, we walked around the house, and I could see a curtain twitching in a window upstairs. Probably the mammy getting a good look at me. But I forgot about her as soon as we came to the yard. Two horses were tied up at a fence beside the stables—a prancing brown horse, pawing the ground and snorting, and standing beside it, half asleep, a big grey with hooves the size of dinner plates. He woke up when we approached and looked at me with huge brown eyes.

"He looks nice," I said to Rory, willing my knees to stop shaking. How was I going to get up on that giant, let alone ride it?

Rory patted the grey horse's neck. "He's a true gent. A gentle giant."

"What about the brown horse?"

"It's a bay. That's what we call a brown horse with a black mane and tail. And this one is a mean bastard but a hell of a hunter. He'll jump a seven-foot bank, no problem."

"Ah. Okay. Bastard bay horse."

"He's called Bertie. After a very famous politician."

I laughed. "Perfect name for a mean bastard horse."

"I knew you'd like it."

An Irish setter appeared from one of the stables, its copper fur gleaming in the evening sun. "Is that Nellie?" I asked as Jake poked his nose at the other dog.

Rory nodded. "Yes. Come here, Nellie, and say hello to a new friend."

Nellie trotted forward and sniffed at Jake, wagging her tail. The two dogs sniffed at each other in that doggy who-are-you kind of way.

"They seem to like each other already," I remarked.

"Yes, they do. Look, I think it would be better to leave your dog with Nellie. He's too young to know how to keep out of the way of horses."

"That's fine." I wiped my sweaty hands on my jeans. Maybe I could stay in the stables too?

Rory locked the dogs into one of the stables. Then he turned his attention to me. "I'll give you a leg-up."

I backed away. "A what?" But before I could escape, Rory had grabbed me and thrown me onto the back of the big grey horse. I wriggled onto the saddle, gripped the horse's warm flanks with my legs and grabbed the reins.

"Don't pull at the reins," Rory ordered. "Hold on to the martingale."

"The what?"

"The strap on his neck. You don't need the reins. He'll follow Bertie. Just stick your feet in the stirrups and we'll get going."

I let go of the reins and took a hold of the strap, groping for the stirrups with my feet while sweat broke out on my upper lip. At the same time, Rory jumped up on Bertie and started to walk away, Charlie following at a leisurely pace. I relaxed and started to enjoy the feeling of riding the big animal, whose gait was surprisingly comfortable. It was like sitting on an undulating mattress.

"Giddy up," I said in attempt to communicate with the animal. He flicked his ears and lumbered forward, me hanging onto the neck strap for dear life.

"What's he doing?" I panted.

Rory looked at us over his shoulder. "He must have thought you wanted him to trot."

"How d-d-do I-I-I s-stop h-h-him?" I wheezed as Charlie increased his speed and Bertie started to do a kind of bunny hop on the spot with excitement.

"Take the reins and pull gently," Rory said as he tried to calm Bertie who was trying to break into canter. "Say something soothing."

I scrambled for the reins and gave it a little tug. "Whoa, you beast."

Charlie came to a dead stop, which made me shoot forward, my arms around his neck. "I didn't mean for you to stop so suddenly," I muttered, fighting to regain my seat in the saddle.

Rory burst out laughing while he was trying to calm his dancing horse. I had to admit he was a superb rider. He didn't look the slightest bit perturbed as he fought to get the better of the overexcited Bertie, who was trying his best to rid himself of his master. Rory finally won and Bertie slowed to a walk beside Charlie.

I'd managed to sit up and get my feet back in the stirrups. I pushed up the riding helmet that had slipped over my eyes. "This is not an easy sport."

Rory leaned over and patted Charlie's neck. "No. It takes quite a lot of practice. But Charlie knows how to handle a beginner, don't you, Charlie?"

We came to gate, and Rory leaned over to open it, letting me through ahead of him. Then we rode down a steep hill overlooking a field with a river running through it.

"Our inch," Rory said. "That's what we called a floodplain like this."

I looked along the river meandering through the landscape, lined with willows dipping their branches in the water. A heron rose suddenly and flew along the river, its large wingspan reflected in the still water.

"Lots of wildlife here, I see."

Rory reined in his horse. "Yes. I keep it as a kind of conservation area. I never let cattle graze here. It would damage the delicate flora and fauna. A waste of good land, but I feel it's important to protect our environment in some little way."

"Unusual for a farmer," I said.

"How do you mean?"

"Farmers don't usually worry about the environment, do they? Take all that slurry you keep spreading for a start. It's full of methane, which is part of the gases that have contributed to global warming. Plus, it seeps into the ground and affects the water we drink. But the farmers don't seem to know anything about that."

Rory frowned. "We all have to earn a living, you know."

"And wreck the environment at the same time?"

He shrugged. "There's no real proof that slurry plays a part in that."

I felt a red-hot ball of anger burn in my chest. "What the hell do you mean? It's well-known that methane emissions from cattle are one of the main contributors to greenhouse gasses."

"Let's drop it, okay? It's too nice an evening to argue."

"Fine," I snapped, annoyed I'd raised the issue. It was a bugbear of mine, but I knew doing anything about it was an impossible task. And this was the wrong time to start complaining about farmers and what they did to the environment.

"I don't spread slurry on my farm, in any case," Rory remarked. "I actually agree with you."

I glanced at him and saw he was trying not to laugh. "Why didn't you say so in the first place?"

"Just to get a rise out of you. I love it when you scowl like that."

"Oh, please. Shut up."

"Okay." He closed his mouth but kept shooting me amused glances, which made me feel both stupid and confused.

We rode on along the river in silence, and the peace and tranquillity of the beautiful place had a calming effect on everyone. Even Bertie relaxed and lowered his head, trying to snatch some grass here and there. The soft breeze cooled my hot cheeks, and I breathed in the sweet smell from the flowering laurels. The swallows swooped around us, and the sun dipped behind the oaks on the hill. Rory turned Bertie around.

"We'd better get back. I know my mother's laid the table for tea."

I suddenly felt a nervous flutter in my stomach. "Your mother?"

"Yes. She wants to meet you. Says she wants to see the famous reporter in the flesh and pick your brain."

I tried to think of a plausible excuse—like a prior engagement—but came up with nothing. What else would I be doing on a Monday evening in Cloughmichael? "Looking forward to meeting her," I said, trying to sound as if I meant it, instead of wanting to jump into my car and drive away as fast as I could.

Rory glanced at me. "Don't worry. She doesn't bite."

I forced a smile. "I'm sure she's lovely."

But when I came face to face with her, I realised at once that 'lovely' was not a word you'd use to describe Breda Quirke.

CHAPTER 9

Rory led the way into a utility room, where we kicked off our boots and washed our hands. Nellie and Jake milled around us and Jake growled at a large tomcat sitting on the window sill.

"The dogs have to wait here. My mother doesn't approve of animals in the house," Rory said.

"What about cats?" I asked.

"Cats are fine. They keep away the mice."

After we'd cleaned up, we continued into a big farmhouse kitchen, where a smell of newly baked bread and sausages frying on the stove made my stomach rumble. We continued into a sunroom, where a table was set with what I guessed was the 'good' china and silver cutlery. Rory pulled out a chair for me. I sat down, putting a starched linen napkin in my lap.

"This looks lovely."

"My mother does a fantastic high tea." He sat down, only to shoot up again as a tall woman came into the room carrying a teapot and a basket of bread. "And here she is," he said. "Mam, this is Finola."

The woman put her burden on the table. "I can see that. Hello, Finola."

I got up and held out my hand. "Hello, Mrs Quirke."

"Please, call me Breda."

As she came around to the other side, I could see her clearly in the bright sunlight streaming in through the windows. She was not at all the oldish woman in a tweed skirt and sensible shoes I'd imagined—far from it. She had the same grey eyes as Rory, but the resemblance ended there. Breda Quirke didn't have her son's charm or good looks. Dressed in jeans and a green cashmere sweater, she was tall and rangy with a weather-beaten face, thin lips, with the voice of a seasoned smoker. There was more than a sprinkle of grey in her short wiry hair, and I could feel callouses in her hand when she gripped mine in a firm handshake.

She looked at me for a moment with her laser eyes. "So, Finola. You've just arrived in Cloughmichael?"

I tried a winning smile as I eased my hand out of her grip "A couple of weeks ago, yes."

"I haven't seen you at mass."

I squirmed. "No, er…"

She pinched her lips. "Not a mass-goer, are you?"

"Not really, no."

"I see." She pulled out a chair. "Let's sit down and eat."

I plopped down on the chair Rory pulled out for me. My knees had suddenly turned to jelly, which wasn't due to my debut on a horse.

Breda kept looking at me. "Did you enjoy riding Charlie?"

"Very much. First time ever on a horse, so it was a bit nerve-racking."

"With your history, I wouldn't say it was that much of a challenge," Breda Quirke remarked. "I read that piece about you in the paper. Rory, go get the rest of the tea while I chat to Finola. It's all in the oven."

"Okay, Mam." Rory went out to the kitchen and returned minutes later with a platter laden with sausages, bacon, grilled tomatoes, roast potatoes and black pudding.

"Just a small tea," Breda said and passed me the platter.

"Help yourself." She poured tea into our cups and handed around a jug of milk.

When we'd all helped ourselves, Breda turned her attention back to me. "So, Finola. Tell me, what made you give up and run away?"

I coughed, nearly choking on a piece of sausage. "Run away? I don't feel I did."

"Looked like it to me. I was disappointed when I saw you were no longer writing for The Irish Telegraph. There was so much more you could have fought for. I came to rely on you to reveal the dirty side of every political party. I thought you'd be our watchdog."

I put down my knife and fork. "You know what, Breda? Being a whistle-blower is a tough job. Nobody really likes us. You have no idea how much hate mail I got after the last scandal was revealed. I had to change my phone number and email address, and close down my Twitter account. That, on top of the fact that the…some people at the top of the media circus were constantly trying to silence me, made it impossible for me to continue. The stress was killing me, and I had some kind of breakdown as a result. It's all very well going out there and pointing the finger, but there comes a time when you have to stop." I drew breath and put another piece of sausage in my mouth. "These are good," I mumbled through my mouthful.

Breda and Rory stared at me for a long time. Then Rory let out his breath. "I had no idea it was that bad," he said.

But Breda wasn't giving up. "Well, you could have taken a break and then gone back."

"I certainly could not," I retorted. "I'm getting too old to be a rebel. I'm here now and I'm going to stay. So there," I added childishly, nearly sticking my tongue out at them.

Breda exchanged a glance with Rory. "You mean you're not going to deal with certain…problems around here?" she asked.

I looked at her squarely. "I'm not going to stir up trouble, if that's what you mean. But what I will do is turn The Knockmealdown News into the most popular newspaper around here. And here's another thing…we're planning to have an online forum on our new website, so anyone who wants to air their grievances can do so. Within reason, of course." I only made that up, but as the idea formed in my mind, I realised it would be a great way to raise our profile.

"So anyone can go there and have a good rant?"

I nodded. "Yes, that's the idea."

Breda's face brightened. "That's very good news indeed. Give me a shout when the forum is up."

"You'll be the first to know."

Rory burst out laughing. "Why do I have a feeling that nothing will be the same in this town ever again?"

"I hope you won't wreck the good old Knockmealdown News, though," Breda said.

I shrugged. "Nothing much to wreck. It was a pretty pathetic little rag when I arrived. May I have some more tea, please?"

Breda lifted the teapot. "But I liked it the way it was. Don't tell me you're going to turn it into Hello Magazine."

I laughed. "Not a bad idea, Breda. I might have a celebrity section. You want to be in it?"

Breda refilled my cup. "I don't really qualify. I'm not a celebrity."

"I've heard there will be some real celebrities around here soon," Rory interrupted. "Some Hollywood movie company is shooting a movie here in the summer."

I nodded. "They're already here."

Rory reached out for a slice of bread. "Hollywood comes to Cloughmichael."

I laughed. "Great headline. May I use it?"

"Of course."

"We're running an ad for extras on Thursday," I continued. "Locals only, they said, or we'll be overrun by wannabe actors from all over the country."

Rory smirked. "There's your chance to become a celebrity, Mam."

"Don't be silly." Breda got up. "I have to go. There's a meeting of the tidy towns committee tonight in the church hall."

"Tidy towns?" I asked. "When will the judges come here?"

"Sometime in the summer," Breda replied. "So we need to get everything in order and get the flower beds and hanging baskets organised. We need volunteers. There's a lot to be done in a very short time. Maybe you could put in a snippet about that in the paper, Finola? Johnny always helped us with that."

"Of course," I promised. "It's a pity Johnny left in such a rush. I'd have loved to have some notes from him about those things."

"Yes. A great pity." She paused. "But it was impossible for him to stay."

"Why?" I asked.

Breda shrugged and again glanced darkly at Rory. "Not for me to say."

I gave up. "I don't even have a contact number for him. Do you?"

"I don't think so." She shot Rory another conspiratorial look. "Do we, Rory?"

"No." Rory rose and started to collect plates and cups. "You go on, Mam. We'll tidy up here."

Breda hesitated. "Don't break anything."

I got up and piled everything on the tray. "We'll be careful."

"The china has to be washed by hand, not in the dishwasher."

"Okay," Rory and I said in unison.

"I'll be back around half past nine."

Rory sighed. "I know. Go on, now, or you'll be late."

Breda nodded. "I'll be off, then. Bye, Finola. It was real pleasure to meet you," she said as if she really meant it.

I smiled and nodded. "Lovely to meet you too. Thank you for tea. It was all delicious."

When Breda's car rumbled up the lane, I carried the tray into the kitchen and put it on the table.

Rory followed with the rest of the tea things and filled the sink with hot, soapy water. "We'd better wash the cups and saucers by hand. But the rest can go in the dishwasher."

I grabbed a tea towel. "I'll dry."

We washed and dried in silence until all the fine china was safely in the china cabinet on the far wall. Rory muttered something as he closed the cabinet door.

"What?"

"I think she liked you."

"Even though I don't go to mass?"

"Yes. She was just trying to make you uncomfortable."

"I gathered that. But I liked her too. She seemed a bit apprehensive of me at first."

"Well, you know, she adheres to the three rules single farmers are always taught by their fathers."

I stared at his back. "What rules?"

He turned around and looked at me in a way that was hard to decipher. "One, don't tell her you own property. Two, don't give her a gift that isn't edible, and three, don't put anything in writing."

I laughed. "I'm not after you or your farm."

"How does she know? I think she was scared of you."

"She didn't look scared."

Rory's eyes darkened. "She's scared of losing me. I'm all she's got. Everyone else has left."

I hung the towel on the rail of the Aga. "Everyone else?"

He turned his back to me while he loaded the dishwasher.

"Yes. My dad died last year. He had Alzheimer's. It was a long, slow process. My two sisters live in Dublin, and my older brother died in a farm accident when he was eighteen. Mam was so brave through it all. She always supported me when I went into politics and even campaigned for me around here. Now that I'm back farming, she's very happy. But she's worried I'll get married, and—"

"And that the new wife will turf her out? That would be a bit cruel, wouldn't it?"

Rory straightened up. "Can you imagine living with your mother-in-law? Especially one as opinionated and domineering as my mother?"

I sank down on a chair. "I can see that would be a problem."

"Yes, it would be. And it has wrecked a few relationships for me. But I love this farm, and I don't want to leave it."

"It's a beautiful place. How long has your family been here?"

Rory pointed out the window. "See that ruined tower over there behind the barn?"

I looked out at the tower, its jagged edges outlined sharply against the blue sky. "Yes. It's the remnant of a Norman tower, isn't it? Eleventh century?"

"That's right. We've been here, on this land, since then."

"Oh." It suddenly struck me that Rory was part of this landscape almost as if he was physically fused to it. He'd never leave or turf his mother out to some little cottage somewhere. That was some challenge for any woman he'd get involved with. I looked at him in awe. "I didn't realise you were that old."

He laughed. "I'm only thirty-nine."

"I didn't mean in that way. I meant your family." Now that Breda had left, I decided to confront him. "So now that we've sorted out your heritage, there's another thing you need to tell me."

"What's that?"

"Don't act the innocent." I fixed him with my gaze, my arms folded across my chest. "Rory Quirke, you're going to tell me about Johnny Keegan and why exactly he left so suddenly. And please don't say you don't know, because you'd be lying."

Rory blinked. "What do you mean?"

"I saw you and your mother exchange looks all through the meal. I'm not an eejit. I know something went on with Johnny. Something serious. But every time I ask a question, people slide away, whistle a little tune and change the subject. Jerry, Miranda, Jules, and now you and Breda. The only one who was honest was Fergal."

"Fergal? What did he say?"

"Don't look so startled. He didn't say much. Only that he didn't know. But he and Johnny were friends, so he'd have told Fergal if he'd been around, but he wasn't because it was foaling season at the stud." I drew breath.

Rory looked at me thoughtfully for what seemed like an hour. I tried to decide if I should walk out or shake him until he spilled the beans. But I waited while he seemed to struggle with himself. Then he went to the cupboard over the sink and took out a bottle of Paddy's and two shot glasses.

He sat down and poured us both a stiff drink. "I think we need this before I tell you."

"Is it that bad?"

"Yes." He knocked back his whiskey in one go, took a deep breath and finally spoke. "How do you feel about bullies?"

"In general? They make my blood boil. So this is about bullying? Johnny was bullied? By whom?"

"Not Johnny. His stepson."

I stared at Rory, my mouth open. "In school, you mean? But couldn't he report it to the headmaster?"

"It was a lot more serious than that. It was everywhere, but not in school. On the Internet, by phone, on the way home, everywhere but school where it would have been noticed. Physical and mental abuse of a twelve-year-old boy by a gang."

I took a gulp of whiskey. "Holy shit. How awful. But who...I mean why couldn't it be stopped?"

"Because of the people involved, Johnny said. He didn't tell me who these people were or to whom they were connected. He didn't want anyone to get hurt."

"So he didn't want to stay and fight them?"

"Too powerful, he said. Jules put them up at the cottage a couple of nights before they left. Johnny, his wife and son. Then they left. I don't know where they went."

"Bloody hell." I couldn't get my head around what Rory had just told me. Bullying of that magnitude in this sleepy little town?

"Yeah," he said as if reading my thoughts. "Nasty things go on under the pretty surface in this place."

"I must find Johnny. Do you have any idea where he went?"

Rory topped up his glass. "None whatsoever. He could have gone to England for all I know."

"But we have to get to the bottom of this. I mean those kids, or whoever they are, must be stopped."

"Of course. But there's a wall of silence around them. The school said they knew nothing about it. It wasn't happening on their premises. The Guards said there was no evidence."

"Too cowardly to get involved, I suspect." I drained my glass. "This is pretty outrageous, actually. How can these creeps be allowed to get away with such things?"

Rory looked at me and smiled. "You're getting excited. And I thought you'd given up the crime and punishment stuff."

"Feck off," I spluttered. "This is too serious to leave alone. We have to expose these bastards."

"We? But I left politics. I want peace and quiet too, remember."

"Like hell you do. If you wanted this left alone, you shouldn't have told me. You've been planning to tell me all along, haven't you? I suppose you invited me here tonight for that very reason."

He looked at me long and hard. "No, Finola. I invited you for a very different reason."

CHAPTER 10

The long talk with Rory still running like a movie in my head, I had trouble going to sleep. The revelation that Johnny's son had been bullied by some gang of thugs was disturbing enough, but so was the way Rory had looked at me just before I left. It confused me more than I was prepared to admit.

I couldn't decide how I felt about him. Attracted, yes, but at the same time afraid to get involved. We'd only met a few times and had mostly argued during those brief meetings. But during those arguments, there was a buzz between us I couldn't deny. *Don't go there, Finola*, I told myself. I'd been hurt so many times, and I didn't want to go through all that again. In any case, if he was looking for a relationship, I wasn't what he needed. And his mother and the farm and… too much baggage. I pushed those thoughts away, picked up a thriller I wanted to read and went to bed.

At one in the morning, deep into the thriller, I jumped when my phone rang. Who could be calling at this hour?

I groped for the phone and mumbled a sleepy 'hello' without checking the caller ID.

"Finola?"

"Um, yeah?"

"It's Colin. Colin Foley."

I closed my eyes for a moment. Colin Foley calling me in

the middle of the night? This had to be some kind of dream. But that famous deep voice in my ear had to be real.

"Hi, Colin. What's up?"

"I know it's late. But I was hoping you'd be awake. I can't sleep, and I have nobody to talk to."

"Nobody? Gee, I'd have thought you could call just about any woman on this planet and she'd jump at the chance."

"Would you?"

"Jump? No. I'm not your run-of-the-mill teenage fan." I yawned. "Sorry. I've had a long day that included my first-ever ride on a horse and ended in a whiskey-drinking contest with a local farmer."

Colin's laugh was possibly even sexier than his voice. "Who won?"

"He did. I had to drive home, so I left him with the rest of the bottle. In any case, I'm trying to cut down on the booze."

"Why?"

"Just to prove to myself I'm not an alcoholic. And I'm not," I hastened to add. "It was just that whenever I found myself in difficult circumstances recently, I developed some bad habits."

"Been there." Colin sounded suddenly serious. "Easy to open a bottle when you're all alone and feeling low. A glass or five of Merlot can feel like your only friend sometimes."

"Hell, yes. But then that friend ends up kicking you in the butt when the buzz wears off." I moved my legs and moaned.

"You okay?" Colin asked, a hint of laughter in his voice. "Is the whiskey kicking in?"

"No, it's the riding. I never knew I had all these muscles in my legs. But enough about me. You want to talk? So talk. What's bothering you?"

Colin let out a long sigh. "Nothing and everything. I'm a little nervous about this movie. Hollywood's take on the nineteen sixteen rising. I don't want to compromise my country and play a role that would ring false or make some romantic shite out of it."

"I know where you're coming from," I said. "I've seen some cringe-making pieces on the subject that made me want to scream."

"Tell me about it," Colin grunted.

"You'll just have to make the best of it. Who's playing the female lead?"

"Caroline O'Hara. She's an Abbey actress. This is her first film role."

"But she's wonderful." I plumped up my pillow. "Not one of those wannabe film stars."

Colin sighed. "I know. But she's a *serious* actress. She's had roles in all those well-known plays at the Abbey Theatre. Becket, O'Casey, Synge. You know. The Playboy of the Western world. Juno and the Paycock. All the old Irish classics."

I let out a snort. "Oh, yawn. Who really enjoys that heavy stuff?"

"Not me. But it makes her look good. I haven't that kind of experience. After modelling, I had some small parts in soaps and then those action movies. I haven't been in anything worth talking about. Never had an acting class in my life. I just…" he laughed, "use my assets."

"And what's wrong with that?" I asked. "You have a great screen presence. You could sell ice cream to polar bears."

"You saw that commercial, huh?"

"What?"

"I'm kidding. But you never know."

"True." I yawned. "Sorry, I think I'll have to hang up. My eyes are closing."

"I'm boring you."

"God, no. But I'm tired and so, I suspect, are you. Try to get some sleep. We can talk later."

"Okay. You're right. I need to rest. We have a big meeting with the crew tomorrow and then the casting of the extras later in the week. I believe you're running a piece about it?"

"Yes. There'll be a big headline on the front page." I hesitated for a moment. "Um, Colin?"

"Yeah?"

"I hate to ask this but…I'd love to do an interview with you."

"Sure, why not?"

"Could it be an exclusive? I mean like it couldn't be printed anywhere else. It would be terrific for the newspaper."

"I'll have to check with my agent."

"Of course. Let me know when you've spoken to him."

"Her. Godzilla. Scary woman. Night, Finola. Talk soon."

I hung up, put out the light and fell asleep with a silly grin on my face.

* * *

The news hit the headlines in all the national newspapers and other media the next day. Miramax was to make a blockbuster movie in County Tipperary starring Colin Foley and Caroline O'Hara. The title of the movie was Rebel in Love, and would be set just before the Easter rising in nineteen sixteen. The cast and crew were already on location and extras from the local community would be hired in the following few days. Details would follow in the local press.

We followed up with an announcement the following day and then the cat was out of the bag. The town was buzzing with excitement, and our teaser with a promise of an exclusive 'soon' resulted in a spike in circulation. Thanks to Hollywood, we were on our way.

The day the casting crew ran auditions in the community hall, there was a queue around the block, and they were still looking at applicants late into the night. Over a hundred people were hired as extras and many more signed on to be in the crowd scenes. Teenage girls camped on the doorstep of the Bianconi Inn and had to be removed forcibly, and a security company was hired to stop intruders and guard the entrance to Jules's farm. Cloughmichael was becoming the hotspot of Tipperary, maybe even the whole of Ireland.

I didn't have much time to think about anything else, but the Johnny Keegan case was still at the back of my mind. Bullying of that magnitude was a serious issue. I was sure that it was still going on and that any victims were afraid to speak up. How to find them was the problem. I mentioned it to Jerry one afternoon in early June.

He stuck his head into my office while I was writing my notes for the interview with Colin. "Hi, Finola. Am I disturbing you?"

I looked up from my laptop. "Hi, Jerry. Come in. I could do with a break."

He walked in and sat down. "Nice chair."

"Better than the rickety antiques you had. I found that one in Mulcahy's in Cashel. It was on sale so didn't do too much damage to the finances. Hope you don't mind."

"Not at all. We need to update the office. Things seem to be improving lately. Nice work, Finola."

I waved my hand at him. "Not my doing. All thanks to Hollywood. Long may they stay."

He nodded. "Oh yes. But you've done some great things too. Like that fun piece about the tidy towns. And the piece about the auditions was a hoot."

"I'm glad you liked it. Dan's a great asset and Audrey, the new trainee."

"Is that the leggy blonde in the short skirt running down the steps just a minute ago?"

"Yes. We all hate her. Legs to her armpits and a figure to die for. And I thought Barbie had gone out of fashion."

Jerry laughed. "I don't think that will ever happen."

"Neither do I." I picked up my phone. "How about a cup of tea? I'll give Sinead a shout."

"I'd love a cup."

When Sinead had delivered two mugs of tea and a packet of digestives, I got down to business. "Jerry, could you be completely honest with me?"

Jerry put his mug on the desk. "I'll do my best. What's this about? The accounts? I haven't fiddled them, if that's what you're going to talk about. We really did as badly as they say. But now that things have picked up, I've talked to the bank and it—"

"Shut up for a moment and listen," I interrupted. "It's not about the bloody accounts. I know they're all above board. It's about Johnny Keegan's son."

Jerry blanched. "Drago? What about him?"

"Drago? Is that his name?"

"Yes."

"Okay." I finished my tea. "I know that he was being bullied and that it was so serious, Johnny and his family left in a hurry. I also know the bullies in question have some kind of power around here so that nobody dares speak up. I couldn't quite get my head around that such things can be going on in this little town, but I think it's going on everywhere."

"I suppose." Jerry pretended to look out the window, but his hand shook as he picked up his mug.

"You know something about this?"

Jerry looked back at me. "I could say no, but you wouldn't buy that, would you?"

"You bet I wouldn't."

He nodded. "I knew it."

"Tell me what else you know." I leaned back in my chair and put my hands behind my head. "I want you to tell me all you know. I'm all ears."

Jerry looked at the door, then back at me. "It's complicated. And it also involves Aidan, my eldest."

"He's been bullied, too?"

"No, but I think he knows who these bullies are. They haven't picked on him—yet. He and Drago were friends, you see. Drago told Aidan this was going on—about the attacks and threats, both physical and mental. He never mentioned any names, but I think Aidan put two and two together and figured it out."

"But he hasn't said anything?"

"No. Things have been quiet for a while. I think the members of this gang are keeping their heads down. The last attack on Drago was pretty vicious. They broke his arm and messed up his face. That's when Johnny and Madlena decided to leave and go and live somewhere else."

"Where's she from?"

"Croatia. I have a feeling these attacks were of a racist nature."

"Bloody hell." I leaned forward and bored my eyes into his. "Jerry, this has to stop. We have to nail the bastards."

He nodded, looking miserable. "I know. But how?"

"I want to talk to Aidan."

"Okay. I'm not sure he'll tell you anything, but you have my permission to speak to him."

"Good. Could you fill Miranda in on this? And then if I could come to your house and talk to Aidan whenever it suits, that would be a great help."

Jerry got up. "I'll call you."

After Jerry had left, I stared blankly at the computer screen. Aidan obviously knew something, and I was going to do my best to find out what it was. But the person I most wanted to talk to was Drago, who had disappeared so mysteriously. I needed to find him. Someone had to know where they'd gone. I wracked my brain for a while, and then I had an idea. I picked up the phone and punched in a number.

"Hi. Finola here. Tell me, does Johnny Keegan have any family in this area?"

CHAPTER 11

"Kilkenny," I said to Colin that evening when he called. "Want to come?"

"Why are you going there?"

"Research. Don't ask. But I thought, as you said you have a day off, you'd like a break. Kilkenny is a lovely town. Only an hour's drive from here. You could look at the castle while I do my research."

"Why not? If I can sneak off without being seen." Colin sighed. "I'm standing here at the window, looking at five girls pointing their phones at me."

"Must be a pain. Can you sneak out the back?"

"This is the back. I had to change rooms because of the stalkers. These girls climbed a six-foot wall into the back yard."

I couldn't help laughing. "That's the price of fame."

"Yeah, right. I thought they'd give up when they got hungry, but they brought sandwiches. Where are their parents?"

"In the pub, most likely. But if you want to avoid being followed tomorrow, I'll pick you up at seven thirty tomorrow morning. They'll be fast asleep then. Sorry, Colin, I have to go. I have an appointment."

"This late?"

"It's only eight. I'm a journalist. We don't have office hours."

"I know. I was only—" He paused and cleared his throat. "Never mind. I'll let you go. Bye for now."

"I'll see you tomorrow, Colin," I said softly and hung up. What was that edge in his voice? Loneliness? Colin Foley, voted the hottest man on earth was lonely? I shook my head and prepared for one of the toughest assignments ever: getting some answers out of a teenage boy.

* * *

The house was quiet when I arrived. Jerry let me in. His face broke into a smile as he caught sight of Jake beside me.

"You brought your puppy."

"Do you mind if he comes in? He's perfectly house-trained. And he won't steal food in the kitchen, will you, Jake?"

Jake wagged his tail and sniffed at Jerry's legs.

"He's very welcome." Jerry rubbed Jake's ears. "He's getting big."

"I know. I think he'll be as big as his dad, whoever he was. Like a giant black springer spaniel. The Labrador part is in his size and appetite."

"He's a lovely fellow." Jerry walked ahead of me into the living room. "We've just finished supper. We didn't tell Aidan you were here especially to see him. I just said you'd be dropping in after work. I thought you could talk to him casually. That way it won't look like an interrogation. And he might open up more to you than he has to us."

"God, Jerry, I have no experience of teenagers."

"He admires you. He read your book and the whole story about that insurance scam. In fact, he's thinking about doing journalism, eventually. Either that or law."

I peered at a framed photo of an angelic-looking boy on the antique table. "I hope he picks law. Is this Aidan?"

"Yes. When he was twelve, at his confirmation. He's grown a lot since then."

"He's the spit of Miranda."

Jerry laughed. "Yes, he got the looks. The other two look like me."

I peered out into the garden, peaceful in the gathering dusk. "It's very quiet. Where is everybody?"

"Soccer practice. It should be over by now. Miranda's gone to pick them up." He walked to the drinks table. "How about a glass of wine? Or whiskey?"

"A cup of tea would be better. I'm getting into the old country habit of drinking tea every half hour or so."

"I know the feeling. I could do with a cuppa myself. I'll make us a pot, and if the lads haven't totally demolished them, I might find some of those chocolate-chip cookies Miranda made."

"Sounds perfect."

While I waited for the tea and possible cookies, Jake settled down on the rug in front of the fire. I wandered around the room looking at photographs and little ornament strewn around here and there, which made up an attractive mishmash of colours and shapes, mirroring Miranda's artistic flair and her feel for spiritual things. Some of the smooth stones demanded I pick them up and feel their silky coolness in my hand, the flowers had to be smelt and the little chime at the door touched to release their tinkle, like the laughter of fairies. What an enchanting room.

I turned as the door opened and a lanky boy peered in. "Finola?" he said.

"Aidan? Hi. Jerry told me you were here."

He shuffled forward with that awkward teenager walk, his face flushed. He held out his hand and shook mine in a limp handshake. "How do you do?" he said.

I shook his clammy hand. "Howerya, Aidan? You're so polite, you're making me nervous."

Aidan let out a nervous laughter. His nervousness was contagious. How the hell was I going to get him to relax?

Jake got up, stretched, yawned and trotted toward Aidan, sniffing at his legs. Aidan ruffled the fur on the puppy's head. "Hi there. What's his name?"

"Jake."

"He's lovely." Then he backed away, laughing as Jake jumped up, trying to lick his face.

"Down, Jake!" I ordered, which had no effect at all. "Let's sit on the sofa, and I'll get him to calm down."

"Oh, okay." Aidan lowered his six-foot frame onto the green velvet. Jake found this delightful, as he now had free range of Aidan's face.

But I tugged at Jake's collar and stared him down. "Jake, sit," I said with a snarl in my voice that made him obey with a hurt look in his eyes. I patted him on the head. "Good boy." Jake sighed and lay down with a thump. "He's sulking." I said.

"What a ham." Aidan's face broke into a brilliant smile that, despite his braces, lit up his face. I couldn't help smiling back. With that smile and those eyelashes, he was going to turn into a drop-dead gorgeous guy once those braces were off.

"He's such a chancer. But I love him. Do you have a dog?"

"No. We have two cats. Mum's a cat-person, she says. I'd love a dog."

"You can come and walk Jake whenever you want."

"That'd be really cool."

"I live in the little cottage at your aunt's place."

"Yeah, I know. That's where Johnny and his family stayed before they left."

I decided to cut to the chase. "You and Drago were friends, weren't you?" I asked as casually as I could.

Aidan looked down at Jake. "We were, yeah," he mumbled. He lifted his head and looked at me with obvious apprehension. "Are you here to ask about the attacks?"

I was going to say something evasive, but changed my mind. This boy wouldn't be fooled easily. I took a deep breath. "Yes, Aidan, that's why I'm here."

"Are you going to write about it?"

I shook my head. "No. I'm not going to write about it as such. But I might do a piece about bullying in general. I've seen a campaign and a website that was started in Sweden. Mostly about cyber bullying of young people. So maybe that's an idea? You could help me and maybe get some of your friends—"

"This wasn't cyber bullying," Aidan interrupted. "Well, some of it was. But it was also other attacks and threats. They—"

"They…who?"

Aidan didn't reply.

I put my hand on his arm. "Oh, never mind. Let's go to *why* instead. What was their motive? Why did they pick on Drago in particular?"

Aidan looked at me with something akin to pity. "Can't you guess? Isn't obvious why they picked on him?"

The penny dropped as I remembered what Jerry had said. "You mean…were these…racist attacks?"

Aidan got up. "Of course they were. Drago is so obviously not Irish. Not just in the way he looks, but the way he speaks English with a strong accent. His mum sounds really Irish, but Drago still doesn't."

I stared at him. "I'm sorry, but I find this hard to believe. Racism? In this nice little town where everyone is so welcoming and helpful? Okay, so they call me a blow-in, but that's just a harmless label they put on everyone who hasn't been here for like five hundred years. I don't like it much, but that's the way it is. I don't find it racist, just a little ignorant."

"Try coming from another country," Aidan shot back. "It's bad enough being a townie and from Dublin. But Croatia?

You might as well be from another planet as far as they're concerned." He plopped back on the sofa and looked at me with despair. "This is actually pretty serious, Finola. These guys…and girls too…are connected to someone who's more than just a school bully. And they're doing it to other foreign students in the town. Not as bad as with Drago, but nasty, anyway. It makes me sick." He sat down again.

"And you can't tell me who he—or they are?"

Aidan hung his head. "No. Do I have to?"

"Not for the moment." I took his hand and squeezed it. "I understand why you're scared. And I suspect you've been threatened in some way. But I'll do my best to help and to get to the bottom of this. And then we'll get together to fight the bullies and the racists. Okay?"

Aidan looked up and nodded. "Okay, Finola. I believe you. You can do anything. You've always been my hero."

It was my turn to blush. "Shucks, Aidan, I'm no superwoman. I just hate bullies, that's all."

"Me too." He jumped to his feet as Jerry came into the room carrying a tray.

I got up. "I'll help you with that, Jerry."

"It's okay." Jerry put the tray on the coffee table. "Go and get another cup, Aidan, if you want to join us. There are even some cookies left."

"No thanks, Dad." Aidan ruffled Jake's fur, and walked to the door. "I have some more homework to catch up on. I have the English exam tomorrow."

Jerry nodded. "Yes. You should do well, though." He turned to me. "Aidan's doing the Junior Cert."

I nodded. "Tough exam. Good luck, Aidan."

"Thank you." He shot me a conspiratorial look. "See ya, Finola. I'll come around and walk Jake whenever you want."

"Terrific. I'll give you a shout."

When the door had closed behind Aidan, and Jerry had poured us both a cup of tea, he turned to me. "So, did he say anything?"

I took a cookie from the plate. "Not much, I'm afraid." I looked at Jerry in silence for a moment and decided not to divulge too much. It was too soon. I needed to have a plan. And when I did, I'd need help. Lots of it. "I don't think he's that involved."

Jerry looked concerned. "Are you sure?"

I was saved from replying by the arrival of Miranda and the boys. Jake jumped up and barked and then ran to jump up on everyone. Miranda shooed them all out into the garden.

She sank down on the sofa. "Phew. Those boys are exhausting. Any chance of a cup of tea?"

"Oops. I think we drank it all." I looked at her pale face and flat hair. She looked exhausted and worried.

Jerry got up. "I'll make you a fresh pot."

"Thanks." Miranda gazed out at the boys running around in the garden throwing sticks at Jake. "We should really have a dog. But I couldn't cope with more noise." She turned to me. "How did you get on with Aidan?"

"Great. We chatted about this and that. And a little bit about Drago."

"And?"

"He didn't tell me much, and I didn't press him. I don't want to upset him during his exams."

"That's very considerate of you." Miranda looked at the door and gestured for me to come closer. "I think it's best to keep everything between the two of you for now, in any case. If Jerry gets wind of something more serious than just a bit of bullying, he might get so upset he'll do something silly. He tends to overreact."

I nodded. "Yes of course. I'll keep this quiet for now. In any case, I don't know much yet. And this is not something I'd run in the paper. I have other plans if it turns out to be what I suspect."

Miranda sighed. "Thank you. Things are bit fraught at

the moment what with Aidan's exams, the boys and our money problems. I'm not sure I could take a lot more."

"You won't have to," I assured her. "In any case, things are looking up at the paper. The circulation's increasing and we have more sponsors."

"That's wonderful." Miranda sat up as Jerry came back in with a mug of tea. "We're so happy you're here to run the paper. Don't know what we'd do without you."

"The paper would be in the toilet, that's what," Jerry muttered as he handed Miranda the mug.

"Toilet paper," Miranda said and started to giggle, which set me off and we both collapsed, laughing hysterically.

Jerry rolled his eyes. "Women," he muttered and left the room.

When we recovered, I wiped my eyes and let out a long sigh. "That made me feel really good. Like going for a run or something."

Miranda finished her tea. "It's good to let off steam. So how was your date with Rory? I heard you met Breda."

"How did you hear this? From Jules?"

"No. Pony-club mother's meeting. Someone heard it at the Tidy Towns committee meeting—or was it the bridge club?" She laughed. "You can't keep anything secret in this town."

"I suppose not," I said while a germ of an idea formed in my mind.

* * *

I picked Colin up from the hotel the next morning. I parked around the back as instructed, and five minutes later, Colin ran through the tall gate, wearing a baseball cap, sunglasses, baggy jeans and a black sweatshirt, neither of which disguised his amazing physique.

"Let's go," he panted, ducking his head while I pulled away from the kerb and drove down the deserted street.

I glanced at him. "But there's nobody around. Those girls must be at school this morning."

"Photographers," he muttered, trying to tune the car radio. "They're everywhere. But they think I'm at Knocknagow, filming, today, so I think we're safe."

"You make me feel I'm in some kind of spy movie." I glanced at him. "Gee, that's a great disguise. Baseball cap and sunglasses. So original. I bet nobody would think of that."

"Ha ha. I know. I didn't have time to go to the disguise shop. Can we get some kind of music on this thing?"

"Why do we need music? It's a lovely drive. We can admire the countryside and talk."

"It's raining."

"It's lovely anyway." I threw a map at him. "You can navigate. We're taking the scenic route. And we'll stop at all the historical landmarks along the way."

Colin groaned. "Why?"

"Because we're Dubliners, and we need to discover the real Ireland."

"Oh, okay."

"Your enthusiasm's killing me. This is our country and we need to discover it."

"That's the real Ireland," Colin said and pointed out the window at two Asian girls waiting to cross the street.

"That's the new Ireland. But you're right—it's also the real Ireland." I glanced at him. "What do you think of that?"

He shrugged. "Fine by me. I'm sure the immigrants work a lot harder than the lazy sods on the dole. Much better for the economy."

"You get a gold star for that answer."

"Thank you, Miss McGee. But don't give me any homework."

We took the Clonmel bypass and turned into the Kilkenny road which wound itself through lovely countryside, with rolling green hills where ruined castles here and there told of a bygone era with a rich history. The summit of Slievenamon loomed above us, the steep slopes of which were a popular climb for hill walkers.

"Slievenamon. The woman's mountain," I said and pointed at the top.

Colin peered up at it. "I can see why it got its name. Looks like a curvy woman lying down. And that pile of stones at the top looks like a nipple of a very large boob."

"Trust a man to notice that."

He laughed and touched my thigh. "You know what, Finola? You're very sexy in a grumpy kind of way."

The car wobbled and I nearly ran into the ditch. "Please don't say stuff like that when I'm driving," I grunted. "And keep your hands to yourself."

"Did it startle you? Or don't men normally say stuff like that to you?" Colin's voice was full of laughter.

I pulled the car onto the hard shoulder and stopped. My hands gripping the wheel, I stared at him for a moment. "What are you doing?"

"I'm flirting with you, Finola."

"Why? Just for fun because you're bored?"

He looked back at me, his eyes earnest. "No, because I find myself oddly drawn to you. I say 'oddly', because you're not like any woman I've ever met. You're not my type or one of those babes I get cast with. But you have something special and unique—honesty, integrity and intelligence. And you're cute with that messy purple hairdo and your freckles and blazing blue eyes. Not to mention your fit but very feminine body." He drew breath while we stared at each other for a loaded minute or so.

I was the first to look away. "Jesus," I muttered, staring out at a ruined church without seeing it. Suddenly furious, I turned back to him. "Why did you have to go and say that, Colin Foley? Now you've ruined what would have been a very nice outing. We've only just met, but I kind of thought we could be friends, crazy as that may seem. But now it's impossible."

He didn't reply. Before I could stop him, he leaned forward and kissed me on the mouth. I pulled away and looked at him, panting hard, as if I'd just run a marathon. Then, before I had a chance to catch my breath, he grabbed me, pulled me towards him and kissed me again, long and hard. This resulted in a clinch and more kissing than I had ever done in my life. It came as no surprise that he was very good at this. I lost myself in his arms and let that beautiful mouth do whatever it wanted: kiss me, make me open my mouth and taste his tongue, then wander down my neck to the opening of my shirt. I finally pulled myself together and peeled his hands off me.

"Please, stop, Colin. We can't…I can't, Oh my God, what's happening?"

"We're having a great ol' snog."

"But we can't. I mean, it's not right."

He pulled me close again. "Why?"

I pushed him away, trying not to be affected by the heat of his body and the smell of him. "Because."

Colin's face broke into a lazy, sexy smile. "Are you afraid of losing control? Of being a woman instead of a hotshot reporter?"

I leaned my forehead on the steering wheel. "I don't know," I mumbled. "But please leave me alone for a while."

He looked out at the empty road and the silent landscape. "You want me to get out? But how will I get back? There's nobody around, and I don't fancy trying to hitch a lift with one of those truck drivers. They might hit on me."

I burst out laughing, sat up and started the car. "No. It's okay. I'm fine. Just don't touch me. We have to get going. I'll drive straight to Kilkenny."

"What about those historical sites and the real Ireland?"

"Go find it on your own. I have work to do."
"Yes, ma'am. I'll try to behave."
"Good."

We remained silent for the rest of the drive. But the atmosphere could have lit a thousand lightbulbs.

CHAPTER 12

By the time we drove down the leafy avenue leading to Kilkenny castle, I'd recovered my calm and my determination not to get romantically or even sexually involved with Colin. It would be hard, but I'd mastered greater challenges.

I pulled up in front of the entrance to the castle. "Here it is. The famous Butlers of Ormonde stronghold."

"Butlers of Ormonde? Who were they?" Colin asked, looking up at the stone walls rising above us.

"Go inside and find out," I ordered. "Visit the castle and walk around the gardens for an hour or two. I'll call you when I've finished my research, and we can go and see the Tudor house in the centre of town."

Colin sighed theatrically. "So much history in one day. I don't know if my tiny brain can take it."

I rolled my eyes. "Do your best. There aren't that many people here, so you might just escape discovery."

"I hope so. Staying incognito is my motto today."

"Good luck."

"See ya later, darlin'." Colin got out of the car, put two fingers to his baseball cap in a jaunty salute and sauntered into the castle.

I sighed and continued down the avenue in search of a parking space, difficult to find in this popular tourist town. But luck was on my side, and I managed to squeeze in between a Volkswagen van with Dutch number plates and a Toyota Yaris from County Meath in the main square.

I didn't have far to go. The address I'd been given was of a small coffee shop just off the main street, five minutes' walk away. It had stopped raining, and the skies brightened as I walked along the wet pavement, past tiny cottages and Victorian houses. I turned the corner and immediately spotted a white cottage with a sign saying Moe's Café over the green door. A bell jingled as I walked into the cosy shop with mouth-watering smells of vanilla and cinnamon and newly baked bread. A grey-haired woman in a frilly apron was arranging buns in a pile behind the counter.

She looked up and smiled as I walked in. "Good morning."

"Hello," I said. "Those buns look good."

"I just made them."

"They smell divine. I'll have one of those and a cup of coffee, please."

The woman nodded. "Sit down by the window, and I'll bring it all to you."

I sat down and gazed out the window while I waited. The street was becoming busy, with tourists and a busload of schoolchildren making their way to the Tudor house across the street.

"Here you go," the woman said as she put a cup of coffee and a bun on a plate on my table.

"Oh, thank you. That was quick." I paused. "Are you Moe?"

"Yes, that's right."

"Moe Keegan? Johnny's aunt?"

She nodded. "I am. Do you know Johnny?"

"Not really, no. My name is Finola McGee, and I took over Johnny's position at The Knockmealdown News when he left."

"Oh." Her face was immediately less friendly and a lot more suspicious. "Who told you where to find me?"

"Fergal O'Hanlon."

"The vet?"

I nodded. "That's right. Johnny's friend." I leaned on my elbows and looked at her pleadingly. "Moe, I need to find Johnny and his family."

She backed away, clasping her hands. "Why?"

"Because I want his help to find the little creeps who bullied his stepson."

"What for? It'll only cause a lot of trouble."

"But if we let them continue, they'll be torturing other young people," I argued.

Moe stood for a moment, looking as if she was trying to decide what to do. "Johnny said he didn't want anyone to know where he went."

I nodded and tore a piece off the bun. "Perfectly understandable. But I'm not anyone."

Moe folded her arms. "You're a journalist."

"Yes, but I don't intend to write about this. Not directly, anyway." I took a deep breath. "Moe, I hate bullies. It's the one thing that makes me see red. And what those shits put Drago through must not go unpunished. They have to be stopped. Don't you see that?"

"I—" The bells on the door jingled and a couple walked in. "I have to go," Moe whispered and regained her place behind the counter.

I sighed and sank my teeth into the delicious vanilla-flavoured bun. Moe was a tough woman to convince. I watched her serve the couple, and then two women and a young girl came in, followed by four German tourists. The café was becoming crowded. Moe wouldn't be available for any more questions.

When I'd finished my coffee, I walked to the counter and asked for my bill. Moe nodded and scribbled something on a slip of paper. I checked the amount. It said seven euros fifty. I was about to dig into my handbag for money when I noticed something else written in small letters at the bottom of the bill. It said "Ahakista."

I looked at Moe. "West Cork? Is that where they are?"

She nodded and took the ten-euro note I handed her. "Yes, but that's all I know."

"Thanks. Keep the change. The bun was delicious."

She nodded, gave me a wan smile and turned to the next customer. I could tell she regretted revealing Johnny's whereabouts.

I looked again at the name on the bill. Ahakista, a small village on the remote Sheepshead peninsula, about four hours by car from Cloughmichael. I'd never been there. Could be a very close-knit community. Would the villagers be willing to tell me where Johnny was living? Not very likely. People in remote areas like that were often suspicious of strangers. But I had to at least try.

* * *

I walked back to the castle, mulling over the morning's event. Annoyingly, the surprise clinch with Colin kept popping up. I just couldn't get the feel of his lips, his hands, his body out of my mind. What female under the age of sixty could resist him? Me, I decided. He was just fooling around, and if I got in any deeper, I'd end up looking like a stupid eejit with a broken heart. I didn't want it broken yet again. Twice was enough, and my first heartbreak had been the one that left the deepest scars.

Eoin, the love of my life, my friend, my soulmate. We fell in love at college and were inseparable for two years, engaged for six months with a wedding planned for after our graduation.

Then he met Orla. How I hated her. Hated her frail little body, her pretty face, blonde hair, sweet voice and gentle ways. She'd stolen my only love with just a bat of her long eyelashes and soft laugh. Eoin had been contrite but adamant. He didn't love me, he said, never really had. Orla had made him realise what real love was. And she wanted a family. I wanted a career in journalism. It was over. Eoin, being a gentleman, put it around that I was the one who'd broken off the engagement. So I was at least spared the pity. I didn't go to their wedding.

Later, we would become friends, and I even came to like Orla. Especially when Eoin was so brutally murdered and I was working on the case. She showed such strength and courage then, and I finally understood why Eoin loved her so much. But the wounds of the broken engagement never really healed.

My second engagement was a huge mistake, from which I walked away with a sense of relief and a feeling deep inside that I'd never have any luck in love.

I promised myself then that I'd only get into a relationship with a man if I truly trusted him. Colin inspired a lot of feelings in a woman, but trust wasn't one of them.

I reached the castle at the same time as the sun broke through the clouds. I walked through the entrance into the gardens, and stopped dead and stared at the scene that met my eyes: Colin, surrounded by giggling women posing with him and taking selfies. Some of them even kissed him. He was laughing and chatting, looking as if he was having the time of his life.

He waved when he saw me. "Hi, Finola!" he called and pulled away from the women. "Excuse me, ladies, my friend wants me."

"Define incognito," I hissed in his ear as the women proceeded to take pictures of us.

He looked only slightly sheepish. "Yeah, well, they were there during the guided tour, and then one of them pointed at me and asked, 'Aren't you Colin Foley?', so what was I supposed to do? Say no, you're wrong, I'm Seamus Moriarty?' In any case, it's good publicity and—"

"And you love the attention, you sneak."

He laughed. "Yeah. Especially with these cute women. They could all be my mother, judging by their looks. Aren't they sweet?"

"Like barracudas. They'll post those selfies on Facebook and Twitter and Instagram and God knows where else."

"Yeah, sure. But that's all great publicity, isn't it?"

"Colin, put your arm around your girlfriend and smile," one of the women called.

Before I had a chance to react, Colin put his arm around me and swivelled me to face the women. He kissed my cheek. They all picked up their phones and snapped away.

I tore away from Colin. "Oh, terrific. Now I'll be plastered on the front page of The Sun as your bloody girlfriend before we know it."

"So what? It's only a bit of fun."

"At my expense. I'd hoped to keep a low profile after all the trouble I've been through." I turned and walked away. "Come on, time to go. I'm parked in the square."

"But what about the Tudor house?"

"I think you've done enough sight-seeing. We'll only run into more of your fans."

"What about lunch? I'm quite peckish."

I stopped and sighed. "We have to eat, I suppose. Maybe we can buy a sandwich and eat in the car?"

"I have a better idea. Isn't Mount Juliet near Kilkenny?"

"You mean the five-star country-house hotel?"

"That's the one. We can have lunch there."

I stared at him. "Are you kidding? The way you're dressed, they'll throw you out on your ear."

He whipped off his sunglasses and beamed at me. "But I'm Colin Foley. They'll let me in naked."

"You'll use your fame to get in? Have you no shame?"

"No."

"Why did I ask?" I muttered and continued through the entrance and down the street, Colin behind me. We reached the square and I got into the car. Suddenly, the ridiculousness of the situation hit me, and I started to laugh.

"What's so funny?" Colin asked getting in beside me.

"Me. You. Us." I turned on the engine. "But what the hell. Let's shake them up at Mount Juliet."

"Now you're talking."

* * *

But instead of invading Mount Juliet, we ended up having a burger at a roadside restaurant. I wasn't the one to chicken out. Colin suddenly got cold feet at the entrance.

"Wait a minute," he said, taking the earphones of his phone out of his ears. "Let's not do this."

I pulled up beside the big gates. "Why not? I was looking forward to seeing their faces when you unveiled your true persona. I could see us being turned away, only to get the best table as you revealed who you were. Egg on the face of the maître d' and all that."

"Yarra bollocks. It's all a load of shite. Let's go back and get a pizza or something."

I sighed. "God, you're such a moody little prima donna. But okay, I was having my doubts about the whole thing, anyway."

"I didn't actually think you'd go for it."

"You were having me on?"

"Yeah." He leaned his head back and tilted the baseball cap over his face. "I'm tired and hungry. Feed me and take me back home, darlin'."

"Okay." I was about to start the car again, when a black Mercedes swept past us through the gates. I caught a glimpse of the two men inside and recognised one of them: Oliver O'Keefe, the politician Rory had introduced me to in the pub that day after my date with Fergal. I didn't know the driver, but Colin did.

He sat up and pointed at the Merc disappearing up the avenue. "You know who that was?"

"Yes. Oliver O'Keefe. Local politician. Big noise in Cloughmichael."

"Not him," Colin argued. "The other guy. That was that gobshite what's-his-name. Head of the Irish Democrats or whatever they're called."

"The new party? They got two seats in the last election."

"They'll get more in the next one," Colin stated. "Just look up their website and read their manifesto. Scary stuff."

I stared at him. "I didn't know you were interested in politics."

"This is my country. I want to know where it's going."

"Good for you. But why did you say the Irish Democrats are scary?"

Colin snorted. "Because they look like bloody Nazis. Thought you might have noticed, being a political reporter and all. The stuff they put out is thinly veiled racism."

"I haven't been in touch with the current trends for a while," I had to admit.

Colin sighed and slumped in his seat. "You'd better catch up. But right now, I'm starving. Take me to some food, okay?"

"Right away, your lordship," I quipped and drove off. It didn't take us long to find a petrol station with a fast-food restaurant attached, where we enjoyed a lunch more to Colin's liking: a cheeseburger deluxe with extra fries and ketchup.

The drive back was not as fraught with sexual tension as I'd feared. Colin spent most of the hour on his phone, taking orders from the production team and his publicist.

The shooting would start the following day, and from then on, I wouldn't see much of Colin, he said.

I didn't know if I was relieved or disappointed. But I knew a time away from temptation would be good for me.

CHAPTER 13

I had to put off my visit to West Cork, as things at the paper got hectic. So many items to cover in a very short time. Not only did we have to write articles about the Tidy Towns committee meeting and their plans to clean up and beautify the main squares and thoroughfares, we also had to cover a whole pile of other events such as the pony-club competitions, the camogie team's forthcoming match in the county championship semi-final, the cub scout charity race and other team sports and school tournaments. Then there was the new Community Alert scheme started by the Guards, the blood-donor campaign and other social services. This was one busy little town.

We worked hard to cover everything and to give it all a fun, new twist in the layout and design of each page. Audrey, despite her ditzy blonde look, proved a terrific addition to our staff, with her talent for writing snappy prose and her great marketing skills. She and Dan were soon a team I came to rely on for nearly every news item.

Then my outing with Colin hit the news.

"You're in Hello Magazine," Sinead panted one morning, her face pink with excitement.

"What?" I asked. "Who?"

"You." She beamed, holding up an issue of said magazine. She flicked through a few pages and then showed me a fuzzy shot of Colin planting a kiss on my cheek in front of a gaggle of women in the gardens of Kilkenny castle. The picture was a little out of focus, but there was no doubt—that woman with the bad hairdo, closing her eyes, being kissed by a Hollywood star was me.

I nearly fainted. "Holy shit."

"And OK Magazine," Dan, who had just arrived, said behind me.

"The Irish Times too," Audrey laughed, showing me the page on her phone.

I felt dizzy. "Shit. I knew this would happen."

"Irish Independent on line one," Mary said from the switchboard. "Will you take it, Finola? They want to speak to you."

"You went out with Colin Foley?" Sinead asked.

"I'll take it in my office, Mary," I said.

"Hi, Finola, I'm Michelle O'Dea, features editor of The Indo," a woman announced. "I think we met a couple of times."

I sank down in my chair. "Yes, we did. What can I do for you?"

"It's about you and Colin Foley. What can you tell us about that picture and the rumours about your involvement with him?"

"No comment," I snapped. "What the hell did you expect me to say?"

She laughed. "Yeah, yeah, I know. But hey, we're colleagues. I mean, just between you and me."

"And the whole country?" I filled in. "Do you really expect me to believe you'd keep whatever I say confidential?"

"Ah, well, no. But the pictures are out there now, and they tell their own story. I'd say the cat is out of the bag whatever you say or do."

"What cat? There is no cat. Colin and I are friends. That's all I'm going to say."

She let out an ironic laugh. "Yeah, right."

"Anything else I can do for you?" I asked sweetly.

"How about an exclusive with Colin?"

"That's already been covered. We have the exclusive. But it won't be published until the movie is out. But—" I paused while I thought. "We're doing a series of articles about the movie as it's being made. Then we're putting it all together into a glossy magazine. But that's confidential, of course."

"Of course. Well," she sighed. "I suppose I can't compete with Colin's new love interest." Before I could protest, she'd said goodbye and hung up.

"Bitch," I muttered.

The phone rang again. This time it was Sharon. "Finola? What *is* this about you and Colin Foley? I just saw it in Closer magazine at the hairdressers. I nearly choked on my skinny latte."

"Oh, that. It's nothing," I said. "It was…Photoshopped."

"What? Photoshopped? Why? By whom?"

"Some kind of joke. Forget about it."

"Weird joke, I have to say," Sharon sniffed. "But how are you, Finola? Enjoying the country and your new job?"

"Immensely. Loving it. I never knew country living was so exciting."

"Really?" Sharon paused. "But I suppose the film crew has glammed up the place a bit."

"Of course. It's a great lift for the town."

"And Colin Foley? Have you met him yet?"

"Um, yes. Briefly."

"You're sooo lucky." Sharon sighed. "I'd come down to visit you if I wasn't so busy. But I might still come later on."

"I bloody hope not," I muttered when she'd hung up.

"What?" Audrey had just walked into the room with a mug of coffee.

"Not you. The woman from The Indo and then my sister-in-law. Tried to milk me for information about my 'love affair', with Colin," I said, making quote marks.

"And…it isn't true?" Audrey fixed me with her huge Bambi eyes.

"Hell, no. He's gorgeous, yes. Flirts with any female who has a pulse. The trick is not to be taken in by it."

Audrey sat down and wound her endless legs around each other. "And you weren't?"

My face felt suddenly hot. "Weeelll…I'm only human. Gotta say, he's very good at it."

Audrey giggled. "I can imagine." She straightened up. "What was that about a glossy magazine?"

"Oh that. I made it up just to flatten your one from The Indo."

Audrey pushed the mug towards me. "But isn't it a great idea? I got you coffee, by the way."

I nodded and grabbed the mug. "Thanks. Yes, you're right. It is. I mean we have all that on our doorstep, so to speak. Especially as I live next door to the big house, where most of the scenes are being shot. And the set's closed to the public. If I can swing it with the director, I could get an exclusive for any pictures."

"They're shooting some crowd scenes in the main square today. Dan could go and take a few shots. Interview the extras and get pictures of them as they're getting into costume and make-up. Do a 'behind the scenes' thing. Then we can put that in the magazine. They'll snap it up and get extra copies for their friends and relatives."

I felt a rush of excitement. "Brilliant. But a glossy will be expensive to produce, I'd imagine."

"Jerry can do the production. Doesn't he publish books?"

"Yes, you're right." I looked at her with respect. "Audrey, you are, without a doubt, a genius."

Audrey shrugged with fake modesty. "Aw, shucks, it was nuttin'. No, actually, you're right. I'm a great, big, fecking genius. I'll probably get the Nobel Prize one day."

I threw a scrunched-up napkin at her. "Get out of here and do some work."

"Yes, sir." Audrey unravelled her legs and got up. "What shall I say when they call from all the other papers and magazines?"

I glared at her. "I'm not in. To anyone."

"Gotcha," Audrey said and disappeared.

My phone rang. I checked the caller ID before I answered. Colin.

"Finola, I only have a minute before we start the morning's shoot."

"I haven't much time myself, so make it snappy."

"Okay. I just wanted to say I'm sorry about that picture. It's doing the rounds, and reporters are going to start pestering you."

"They've already started. But I'm grand. I'm not taking any calls or making any statements."

"Nor am I. Let's keep them guessing. It'll all fizzle out if you don't give them anything to write about."

"I know, sweetheart. I'm a journalist."

"So you are. Okay. If you can handle it, I'm a lot happier."

"You might be happy," I grunted. "I'm bloody furious. I don't *appreciate* looking like a stupid eejit in front of everyone in this country."

"Aw, Finola, you're so cute when you're pissed off like this."

"Feck off."

"I *said* sorry." Colin sounded contrite, but I could tell he was still laughing. "Hey, this is the first time a woman's complained about being seen having a cuddle with me."

"Oh, please." I rolled my eyes and sighed. "You know exactly where I'm coming from, Colin."

"Of course, darlin'. You're a career woman. A reporter with a hell of a track record and you want to be taken seriously."

"I can hear you find this hilarious."

Colin laughed. "Yeah, it is kinda funny when you think about it."

"I'm not laughing." I took a deep breath. "Colin, if you can do anything to kill this story, please do it now"

"Okay, my darling. I'll make a statement, telling the truth."

I let out a long sigh of relief. "Thank you."

"You're welcome. See you soon, I hope."

"Yes. Maybe." As I hung up, I realised, despite my protestations, I did want to see him again. Soon. "Shut up," I muttered to my libido and got back to work.

* * *

Colin's statement hit the news the next day. But it wasn't *at all* what I wanted to see.

"Oh my God," Audrey said when she read it. "I thought you said he was going to put them off."

I tore The Irish Independent from her hand and looked at the short article on the front page with a quote from Colin that said, *My relationship with Finola McGee is private and confidential. I'm asking members of the press to respect our privacy at this time. We will not give any interviews or pose for pictures under any circumstances.*

Audrey stared at me. "What does he mean?"

I threw the paper back at her. "He's taking the piss."

Audrey laughed. "Cheeky monkey." She looked at me thoughtfully. "But I still think he fancies you."

"Great way to show it."

"The gossip press will be hopping after this. He might as well have shouted from the rooftops that you're having a relationship. What are you going to do?"

I sat back in my chair and looked out the window while I

thought. Then I looked back at Audrey. "I'm not going to do anything. Except go away for a few days. Can you and Dan hold the fort here while I'm gone?"

She nodded. "Of course. We can keep to the schedule and put the paper to bed tonight for tomorrow's issue. But then we have the forum that's opening on the website tomorrow. And I'm putting up the Facebook page and getting the Twitter account."

"I'll keep an eye on the forum," I promised. "I can get online from anywhere. I'm the main moderator anyway."

"Where are you going?"

"To the seaside," I said after a moment's deliberation. Better to remain mysterious. The fewer people who knew, the better.

CHAPTER 14

The evening before I left for West Cork, I called on Jules to ask her to mind Jake while I was away. I walked into the warm, cosy kitchen and found not Jules, but Rory.

I stopped dead, Jake under my arm. "Hi. What are you doing here?"

"Having tea with Jules." Rory filled the kettle at the sink. "But she's feeding the horses and talking to the film crew. She'll be here in a minute."

"I thought she was out. There were no dogs outside." I let Jake onto the floor, where he soon joined Nellie on an old cushion in front of the Aga. "Have you seen the top yard? Looks like the back lot of Universal studios. Trailers and equipment and props everywhere."

Rory turned on the kettle. "I know. I had no idea you needed so many people to make a movie."

"They have a catering tent as well. You'd think it was some kind of military campaign."

"It's going to be a little busy around here this summer. I hope Jules won't mind too much."

I looked at his glum face. "What's up? Problems at the farm?"

He shrugged. "Nothing worth mentioning. A bit of a tiff with my mother, that's all."

"About what? You didn't do your homework?"

He shot me a pale smile. "Yeah, right. I suppose it sounds a bit childish to you."

I suddenly noticed he was more than a little stressed. Dressed in crumpled corduroys and a faded blue sweater with holes at the elbows, his hair ruffled by the wind, he looked young and vulnerable and far from the confident country gentleman farmer he had appeared at first.

"I'm sorry," I said. "Didn't mean to sound flippant. I've been a little preoccupied myself, with…er, stuff."

He nodded. "I know. I saw the piece in The Irish Times this morning. So, you're dating this movie star?"

I squirmed. "No, I'm not. He's just trying to annoy me. And I don't want to talk about it if you don't mind."

"So he succeeded?" A teasing smile made his face a little less glum.

"Yeah, sure. He annoyed me big time." I sat down at the scarred wooden table. "But let's not go there, okay? I'm trying to forget it. No big deal. I'm more interested in your tiff with Breda. You feel like talking about it?"

He shrugged. "I don't mind. It'll be all over town soon, anyway. That and your fling with your man. The tongues will be wagging in the pubs tonight." He put three teabags in a teapot. "I presume you won't mind a cup of tea."

"I'm gasping for a cuppa. I thought you'd never ask."

He took out mugs and a milk jug from a cupboard. I couldn't help noticing how at home he was in Jules's kitchen. I got the feeling they were close. But why not? Both farmers, both passionate about horses and dogs, they'd have a lot in common. Maybe they were even involved romantically? Jules was attractive in a wind-blown outdoorsy way. With her toned figure from all that riding and a very cute smile, maybe she was the kind of woman Rory was drawn to? That thought was oddly disturbing.

When we each had a mug of tea in front of us, Rory started to talk. "Okay, so here's the source of the argument—

my plans for a wildlife sanctuary on our land. I want to plant trees and bushes to attract bats and bees and birds and make an area that's free from pollution and chemicals."

Bewildered, I looked at him. "But that's a wonderful idea. What's the problem?"

"Twenty acres of good grazing land. Mam thinks it's a huge waste of fields we should use for grazing cattle. And she's annoyed that I won't build a cesspit and use slurry instead of the old muck spreader."

"Oh God. Doesn't she know anything about protecting the environment?"

Rory snorted. "Environment? She wouldn't know it if she slipped in it."

I had to laugh. "I know what you mean. But you…that's truly wonderful what you're doing."

He shrugged. "I'm not doing it to be wonderful. I love nature and I read about what's happening to this world, how bees are disappearing and land's being poisoned by farming methods. I'd rather live frugally than make money while wrecking the habitats for bees and birds and other wildlife. In any case, if we don't have bees, we won't be able to grow things. I wish that was better understood."

"So do I. Would you like to write an article for the paper about this? We're actually planning a nature-watch section in the next month or so. It would be great to kick it off with something like this. Local farmer's amazing initiative or something…" I trailed off while I imagined the page with a picture of Rory with his dog on the part of the farm that would be the wildlife sanctuary.

"Not so fast," he protested. "I haven't got the go-ahead from my mother to do it yet."

I blinked. "But it's your farm!"

Rory looked into his mug. "No. Most of it belongs to her."

I stared at him. "What? How's that possible?"

He met my gaze, his eyes troubled. "My dad didn't make

a will. So, according to Irish inheritance laws, my mother got two-thirds of the farm, and my sisters and I got the remaining third."

"So you only own a third of a third?"

"That's right. And here's the twist—she's said she'll give me her part of the farm if I marry a woman she approves of."

"And that's not likely to happen any time soon, I suppose."

"No. So far she has not only disapproved but has also wrecked any relationship I got into."

"I see. What a dilemma. You love the farm, and you don't want to leave it. But if you fall in love with someone *she* doesn't like, you'll either have to leave or break up."

"That's it. She has me by the short and curlies." Rory gave me a wry smile. "Sometimes, I'm tempted to tell her I'm gay and my partner will be moving in, just to see her face."

I laughed. "I'd like to see a picture of that. But, bloody hell, what a mean bitch."

Rory sighed. "She's not that bad. I mean, she doesn't realise how it's affecting me. She's scared of losing control."

"I know, but…"

The kitchen was silent while I considered the problem. Rory stirred his tea, the dogs snored, basking in the warmth from the Aga, and a thrush landed in the old apple tree outside the window and started to sing.

I was going to reach across the table and take Rory's hand, but the peace was broken by the arrival of the other dogs ahead of Jules. Jake jumped up and started to bark, and Nellie joined in. Jules, dressed in tattered jeans, a wax jacket and wellies, marched into the kitchen.

She kicked off her boots and threw the jacket on a chair. "Tea," she panted and sank down on a chair. "And bread and marmalade."

"Coming up." Rory went to fetch bread, butter and a jar of marmalade from the counter beside the Aga.

Jules homed in on me. "Hi, Finola. How's tricks? I saw you've become the talk of the town."

I sighed. "Yeah, but it's all lies."

Jules winked at Rory. "That's what they all say."

"Very funny," I muttered into my tea.

Jules put her hand on my arm. "Not to you, I'm sure. Sorry. Didn't mean to upset you."

"Thanks."

Jules nodded and took the mug of tea Rory handed her. "I was just in the front rooms talking to the production team. It's going to be a huge hit, they think. So that could be the reason Colin's making a big thing out you and him. Any publicity is good publicity, especially if it involves Colin Foley and his love life. It'll really put the movie on the map even before it's made."

"What about that Caroline O'Hara?" I asked. "Isn't she the up-and-coming star? What about her love life? Why aren't they making up some kind of affair between her and Colin?"

"Have you met her?" Jules enquired.

I shook my head. "No. I've seen a few photos in various newspapers. Very beautiful in that intense, intellectual, Vanessa Redgrave way."

"I was introduced to her just now," Jules said. "Not exactly a laugh a minute. Cold as a fish. Keeps herself to herself. Never leaves her trailer. She just won't play ball, the producer said. She won't even give an interview or appear at parties. It isn't in her contract, she told him. I doubt you could even pretend there's something between her and Colin."

"But…but," I stammered. "What about the love scenes? How can they look as if they're star-crossed lovers if she's like an ice cube?"

"I think it's called acting," Rory said. "Unlike that photo that said more than a thousand words."

I got up. "Crap. I was screwing up my face and closing my eyes."

"As if in ecstasy," Jules said, her mouth quivering.

"Burton and Taylor," Rory filled in. "Everyone remembers their love story. The movie was awful but made millions because of them. It's movie history, not to say a legend. This will be another one."

"Oh please." I threw a piece of soda bread at him.

Jules burst out laughing. "I'm sorry, but it's funny. Finola McGee, the hot-shot crime reporter and the Hollywood star. I couldn't have made that up even if I was drunk."

"Neither could I," I remarked. "And I don't give a shit what people think. I'll just keep my head down and wait for something else to come up that'll take the spotlight off me. In the meantime, I'm going away for a few days. Could you keep Jake for me until Monday?"

"Of course," Jules replied. "No problem."

"Where are you going?" Rory asked.

"Away. Thanks Jules," I said over my shoulder as I left, closing the door behind me to stop Jake following me.

Rory caught up with me when I was nearly at the cottage.

He took my arm. "You're going to look for Johnny, aren't you?"

"How did you know?"

He shrugged. "Just a hunch."

I resisted a strong urge to lean against his solid chest and tell him everything, even ask him to go with me. Not a good idea. "I'm not going to lie. But I'm not going to tell you anything, either. Not yet."

He let go of my arm. "Be careful, Finola."

"I'm always careful."

"Call me if you need help. At any time, wherever you are."

I looked into his earnest grey eyes. "I will."

"Promise?"

I nodded.

"When are you leaving?"

"Early tomorrow morning."

He stepped away. "Okay. Have a good trip. It should be

a nice break, anyway. West Cork is lovely this time of year."

Before I could say anything, he walked away, leaving me looking at his broad back, wondering what else he knew.

* * *

I left early the next morning, deciding to head first to Kinsale at the start of the Wild Atlantic Way, which runs from the southwest all the way up the coast to Donegal in the north. Where had I been the past ten years? I asked myself as the motorway took me through stunning countryside with rolling green hills, steep mountains covered in heather and fields dotted with sheep and cattle. I'd been in Dublin chasing stories, trying to crack down on corruption and lying politicians. Exciting work that had kept me away from discovering the beauty of this small and vibrant country.

I didn't regret the years of hard work, and I was proud of what I'd achieved, but as I drove down the M50, with the gravelly voice of Van Morrison wafting from the loudspeakers, I had a sense of freedom and peace I'd never experienced before.

I drove through the tangle of roads at the Cork City intersection and took a left, past the airport and onto the Kinsale road, through all the little villages with weird names like Riverstick and Inch. Then I arrived at the top of the hill above Kinsale and caught my first glimpse of the ocean. It was a blustery day with dark clouds rolling in from the west. I could see sailing boats leaning over in the strong wind, and little sailing dinghies in the calmer waters of the sheltered harbour. The sun appeared now and then, changing the light from grey to blue, making the waves glitter, then back to grey again. The sky seemed much vaster here, the sea so powerful, crashing onto the rocks below the imposing mass of Charles Fort.

I wondered fleetingly what would have happened if the Spanish had succeeded in beating the English at the end of the sixteenth century as they escaped to Kinsale after the demise of the Spanish Armada. We'd probably all be speaking Spanish. I shrugged and drove on. All so long ago, even if this little fishing-sailing town still bore the marks of that visit by the Spanish navy.

I decided to spend an hour or two there before I continued further west. I had the time, as it would only take two hours to get to my destination. Lunch, I thought, and it had to be seafood. I parked by the harbour wall and made my away along the walkway skirting the waters of the harbour towards Charles fort. The wind whipping my hair around my face and the smell of sea mixed with turf smoke took me back to childhood holidays at the seaside. It made me think of sand castles and ice cream, of sunburnt skin and sausages for tea.

At the end of the walk, I climbed the steep hill and then down a narrow street lined with fishermen's cottages and found what I was looking for: The Bulman, Kinsale's oldest pub with a distinguished culinary reputation. It had even got a mention in the latest Michelin guide.

As I was early, I got a table in a nook by the window, where I could look at the view of the mouth of the harbour and the ocean beyond. I ordered a lobster salad, sat back and finally relaxed, letting my thoughts drift, to the past few days: to Colin, to the paper that was shaping up so well, but especially to Rory. He knew where Johnny was all along. Why hadn't he told me? What else did he know? My phone rang at the same time as my salad arrived.

It was a very breathless Audrey. "Hi, sorry to disturb you. You're not driving?"

"No. Having lunch in Kinsale."

"Oh, lovely." She paused for breath. "I wasn't going to bother you during your weekend away, but I've just had a call from the publicity woman of the movie company. She told me they would be willing to sponsor the glossy mag and will also get some high profile companies to buy ads. They want this to be part of the publicity campaign and a kind of teaser for the movie. And they will let us handle the production and distribution in Ireland, but they'll take care of all international publicity. So this will also be sold in the US. Isn't it fab?" she twittered.

My jaw dropped. "Wow, yes. Amazing. How on earth did you manage that?"

"Oh, well…you know the producer? He asked me to have a drink with him at that cute little pub around the corner… and I kind of threw this idea at him. Didn't take him long to agree."

"I see. Hmm…what did you wear?"

She coughed. "Boots and a skirt."

I laughed. "You mean the thigh-high suede boots and the micro-mini?"

"Yeah, yeah, okay. So I compromised the whole feminist movement. But the end justified the means, big time."

"I agree. I don't have your looks, but if you've got it, flaunt it. What else are assets for?"

Audrey let out a long sigh. "Gee, I thought you'd be annoyed. But hey, it worked. Tough luck on the men who fall for it, right?"

"Audrey, you're one hell of an operator. You'll go far. I only pity the poor men who cross your path." I was still laughing when I hung up. Audrey hid a very sharp brain under that wild blonde head of hair.

I picked up my phone to read the latest news in The Irish Telegraph while I ate the rest of my salad. I noticed the new editor had a decidedly meek tone in her leader. Trying to hang on to her job and not make any waves to annoy the establishment, I supposed. After I'd read the main news, I turned to the rest of the articles, especially the political column, written by Brendan, my ex assistant and confidant. He'd also turned his ass to the wind and took the road of the mainstream. No controversy there, except in the last paragraph, where he cast aspersions on the new party, The Irish Democrats, wondering if they were really serious about the racist slant in their politics.

While it's true that Ireland isn't a rich country, we can ill afford to be negative in our approach to the refugee crisis in Europe. Is this country not better off if we allow integration and open our borders to the less fortunate? The Irish Democrats are out of step with the times. The Irish people need to embrace immigration, not fight it. Weren't we refugees of a kind not so long ago? It's shameful that this party, with its neo-Nazi undertones, is gaining in popularity. Where's the famous Irish welcome?

"Good on ya, Brendan," I said to myself. He was doing it by stealth. The best way to sow discontent.

I paid the bill and set off for West Cork to do my own bit against racism.

CHAPTER 15

Ahakista, on the Sheepshead peninsula sticking out into the Atlantic did not appear to be as remote as the map suggested. The small village overlooking the blue waters of Dunmanus Bay was teeming with people.

"It's our Irish music festival weekend," the hostess of the B and B on the hill told me in her sing-song Cork accent. "Every singer and fiddle player in Ireland is here today. They'll be playing all night in our pubs and in the square too."

"Fabulous," I said, mentally waving goodbye to a night's sleep.

"But we're a little bit away from the village, so I'm sure it won't be too noisy up here," she added, as if she'd read my mind.

I took the key she handed me. "I'm sure it'll be fine. I want to go down there and enjoy the music for a bit, anyway. Is there anywhere I could get a bite to eat?"

"Ah sure, isn't there a seafood buffet laid on in the harbour tonight. All you can eat for twenty euros with a bottle of Harp thrown in."

"Sounds good," I said and went to settle into my room. But I stopped on my way down the corridor. "Oh, by the way…I wonder if you know a friend of mine who lives here…Johnny Keegan?"

She knitted her brows. "Keegan? No, don't think so. Lives here you say?"

"That's right. Just moved here with his wife and son, who's around twelve. His wife is from Croatia."

She brightened. "Oh, you mean Sean. Sean Mac Aodhagáin. He's a writer, and she works in the garden centre. Lovely girl. And their boy…skinny little thing. But he can sing. A voice like an angel, so he has. I believe he'll be singing in The Tin Pub tonight. You'll meet them there."

"Sean Mac Aodhagáin?" I asked, mystified. Then I slapped my forehead. "Of course! That's the Gaelic version of his name. Should have known. Great! Thank you so much." I said and continued to my room.

The room was small but clean, the bed made up with crisp white sheets. The open window had stunning views over the bay and the mountains on the far side. I leant out to enjoy the scenery and the soft breeze on my face. I took a deep breath of the clean air and felt suddenly invigorated despite the long drive. Such a heavenly place. I wished, for just a moment, I'd come for a weekend break with no other agenda than to have fun and discover this wonderful area. But I had work to do and couldn't afford to linger. In any case, I couldn't imagine a more pleasant environment for a little sleuthing. I tore myself away from the view, tossed my bag on the bed, ran my fingers through my hair and set off for the harbour and the seafood buffet.

* * *

The wind had dropped, and the ocean lay like a mirror all the way to the horizon, the evening sun reflected in its silvery-blue surface. The light had a golden hue, the sky streaked with wisps of pink and red. There was hush at the harbour, where someone was strumming a guitar. A small group of people had already arrived, helping themselves to the food laid out on trestle tables along the harbour wall.

I handed my twenty euros to a girl at the near end of the buffet and picked up a plate, my mouth watering at the sight and smell of the many kinds of seafood: shrimp, mussels, deep fried baby squid, lobster tails, smoked salmon and crab claws. I took a little bit of everything, including potato salad and a thick slice of soda bread and grabbed a bottle of Harp. I looked around for somewhere to sit and was invited to join a group of French tourists at one of the long tables set up along the far wall. But I smiled and shook my head. I didn't want to be trapped into long conversations. I felt sure Johnny and his family would come to the buffet before the music started. They would feel safe and welcome here.

My hunch proved to be correct. I'd just sat down at the end of an empty table, when I spotted a stocky man with fair hair walking hand-in-hand with a slender dark-haired woman. Behind them a dark-skinned boy of around ten with black curly hair ambled along, kicking stones, his hands in the pockets of his jeans. I'd seen a photo of Johnny in the archives, so I knew it was him. And the woman, with her dark hair and Madonna face, answered the description of his wife exactly.

The group came closer and was greeted by the locals gathered at the buffet table. Handshakes, kisses on the cheek and claps on the back. The boy's hair was ruffled by more than one person. This made him smile shyly and edge closer to his mother.

I decided to make my first move and stood up as they approached my table.

"Is anyone sitting here?" the man asked.

"No," I replied, "I'm the only one here. I have that effect on people."

The man laughed. "We'll join you, so. Madlena," he called to the woman. "Come and sit here. Plenty of room."

The woman joined us, her son at her side. She put her plate on the table and held out her hand. "Hello," she said. "I'm Madlena and this is my son, Drago." She had a melodious voice with a surprisingly strong Irish accent.

"Hi," I said, taking her cool slim hand. "My name is…" I paused. "I'd better come clean. I'm Finola McGee, the new editor of The Knockmealdown News."

The man stared at me for a full minute. "I see," he said coolly. The friendly look in his eyes was instantly replaced by suspicion and a hint of contempt. "You're looking for a story? Sorry, but we're not going to give you one." He backed away.

I put my hand on his arm. "Hey, don't walk off like that before I've had a chance to explain. I'm not looking for a story, I swear."

He made a sound halfway between a grunt and a laugh "Yeah, right. Finola McGee came all this way for a bit of sightseeing? Pull the other one. I know your reputation." He leant forward, glaring at me. "Listen, we don't want any trouble or need any help. We came here for a peaceful life among nice people, and that's what we got. We're trying to move on from something very painful, especially for our son. Leave us alone, okay?"

I let my hand fall, hit by a dart of shame. Why had I travelled all this way to find these people? Was the pursuit of a story so hardwired into my brain that I bulldozed over everyone with no regard for their feelings? But in this case, I told myself, I wasn't looking for a story, but for justice and to try to stamp out a fire before it spread and engulfed all of society.

Johnny was still staring at me, his eyes like granite. "Johnny," I started. "I know something awful was going on in Cloughmichael before you left. But…" I ran my hand through my hair. "This is hard to explain. My coming here is not about writing a sensational story to sell copies. There's enough other stuff going on in the town right now to fill every issue until Christmas, believe me. What I want to do is to find the bullies and make them stop. I have a feeling the…the attacks on your son were about racism, and that it's connected to something far more serious than just a bit of bullying by kids." I drew breath.

Johnny sank down on the bench and glanced at Madlena. "Okay. Go on."

I didn't quite know what to say next. All around us, people were eating and drinking beer, chatting and laughing. The sun was dipping into the still ocean, the plaintive cries of seagulls filled the air, and in the distance, the lilting sound of a tin whistle added to the feeling of peace and tranquillity.

"It's a stunning evening," I said. "It feels wrong to talk about all this right now."

Madlena nodded. "Yes, you're right." She glanced at Johnny. "I believe Finola. And I think she's right. We shouldn't stick our heads in the sand. What is that quote you read to me the other day, Johnny? About the forces of evil triumphing or something?"

"'All that is necessary for evil to triumph is that good men do nothing,'" I said. "Edmund Burke. Irish politician and philosopher. And wasn't he right?"

She nodded. "Oh yes. But when you're up against evil, running away's the easiest option."

Drago, who had remained quiet during the conversation, his dark eyes darting from one to the other, suddenly spoke. "I don't want to go back. I want to stay here. I like this place. There's so much music. And nice guys to hang with."

Madlena put her arm around her son. "We're not going back. This is our home now."

"And tonight we'll just have fun," Johnny added. He looked at me, his eyes a little less hostile. "I'd be willing to talk tomorrow. This thing has been on my mind ever since we came here. And you're right, Madlena. If we do nothing, evil will triumph."

Madlena nodded. "We have to do something, even if it's just sharing what we know with Finola. But not tonight." Her smile was radiant as she looked at her son. "Drago's going to sing in the pub with the local band. It's a big night for him. Will you join us at The Tin Pub to hear him, Finola?"

"I'd love to. I have a feeling I'll be in for a treat."

CHAPTER 16

I was right. Later, at the quaint Tin Pub, a tiny bar made completely out of tin, Drago's performance stood out among all the others. Pressed against the wall, I nursed a pint of Murphy's, the Cork equivalent of Guinness, and listened to possibly the best Irish music session in the country.

And then, Drago. The performance of that young boy silenced the packed pub. A voice like that of an angel, accompanied by the tin whistle and the fiddle, stopped all conversation. In the ensuing silence, Drago sang his heart out, and soon there wasn't a dry eye in the pub. He went through a long repertoire of classic Irish ballads, ending with a beautiful rendition of Danny Boy, the song that always brought me out in goosebumps. This was no exception.

When the last note hung in the air, there was a long silence, broken eventually by applause, whistles and shouting. Drago bowed with the grace and modesty of a seasoned performer, and then the fiddle player struck up a toe-tapping jig.

Someone touched my shoulder. I turned and saw Johnny. "What did you think?"

"Outstanding," I said.

He nodded and smiled. "I know. Can I get you a drink?"

I lifted my glass. "Thanks, but I think I'll just finish this and then head for bed. It's late and I've had a long day."

"Okay. We won't stay long either. We'll be going home as soon as we've pulled Drago away from his fans. But we need to talk."

"Yes, we do," I agreed. "How about we meet for coffee tomorrow? Isn't there a little coffee shop near the garden centre?"

"Yes. I'll meet you there at around eleven. Drago and Madlena are going on a boat trip, so it'll be just me."

"That's fine. Maybe better if it's just the two of us."

"Could be. Goodnight, Finola. See you tomorrow." Johnny disappeared back into the throng.

After a short conversation with two Dubliners on a walking holiday, I finished my pint and walked up the hill to my lodgings, that bed with cool sheets the only thing on my mind. As I walked up the hill, I could still hear the music mingling with the soft whisper of the breeze and the sudden screech of an owl. A full moon was reflected in the black waters of the bay, like a large eye looking down from heaven. I'm not religious, but I sometimes feel a spiritual presence, and that was such a moment. I stopped, just to let myself take in the beauty of the night, the faint smell of salt and seaweed, and the cool air against my hot face.

My phone pinged. I looked at the text. It was from Colin. **Where r u? Thought we could go for a drink?**

I turned on sleep mode without replying. I didn't need that kind of distraction.

* * *

I woke up the next morning to discover a soft mist enveloping the bay, accompanied by a fine drizzle that made everything damp, turning my hair into frizzy purple wire. But that was the least of my worries. I was about to find out what had happened to make Johnny flee from Cloughmichael.

My belly full of award-winning Irish breakfast, I made my way down the hill to the little coffee shop beside the gardening centre.

Johnny was already sitting at a round table by the old sash window, a big cup of coffee and a scone slathered with cream and jam in front of him.

I pulled out the other chair. "Good morning."

He didn't look up from his phone. "Morning," he grunted. "Sorry. Just looking up the papers. It's an obsession I have."

"Once a journalist, always a journalist." I lifted a hand to attract the attention of the girl at the counter. "Could you bring me a cappuccino, please?"

"Right away," she replied with a cheery smile. "Anything to eat? The scones are just out of the oven."

"No, just the coffee, thanks."

"You sure?" Johnny asked after the waitress had left.

I sighed and touched my stomach. "I can't eat anything. I just had a gargantuan breakfast at the B and B. Couldn't resist the smell."

"I know what you mean," Johnny said. "Their breakfast is famous. Did you have the home-made sausages?"

"Yes," I groaned. "And the black pudding, the eggs from their own hens, the rashers, the…oh God, I don't want to think about it. What is it about a full Irish that's so tempting?"

Johnny cut a bit off his scone. "Something to do with childhood memories. You know, the seaside holidays, staying in guest houses with your family and stuffing yourself with fried sausages and eggs and porridge before you braved the Irish summer weather."

I laughed. "Oh yeah. The wind and rain and then going to the beach whatever the weather because we were on holiday." I sighed. In those early days of childhood, my parents were still happy, and my dad hadn't come up against the nasties of this world which, in time, turned him into one of them.

The Blow-In

Johnny ate half his scone before either of us spoke. I didn't want to start pushing him. I thought it better to let him tell his story his own way. So I waited and sipped my coffee and looked out across the bay.

"Nice soft day," I said to break the silence.

Johnny turned his attention from the scone. "True. That mist makes everything look soft." He took a deep breath and squared his shoulders as if bracing a strong wind. "So," he started. "I'd better fill you in on what happened."

"Only if you feel like it."

"I don't. But Madlena's right. The truth has to come out. I just don't want Drago hurt again."

"Of course you don't. And he won't be," I assured him. "There's no need to involve him. I just need to know the facts and who we're up against."

Johnny looked puzzled. "What are you planning to do?"

"You first. Tell me what happened."

Johnny pushed away his plate. "It's rather a long story. I'll try to make it as short as possible."

"Okay. Go on," I said, my impatience mounting to a crescendo.

Johnny nodded. "As you know, Madlena and Drago are originally from Croatia. Dalmatia, to be exact. We met when I was on holiday there and spent a week on an island called Hvar about eight years ago. Gorgeous place. Madlena and I met at a bar in the harbour of the small village where she lived. She was a widow with a little boy. She was out with a group of friends, and somehow we got chatting. She asked me where I was from and all that. She was interested in Ireland and wanted to go and see it. Then we fell in love, and she came to Cloughmichael a few months after that. We were married the following spring, and Drago went to the little primary school next door to the church. You know where it is?"

I nodded. "Yes. Quite near the office."

"Nice little school." Johnny paused for breath. "All was well the first few years. Madlena got a job and took a course in horticulture. She loves gardening. Drago was getting on well, too, and was looking forward to secondary school when he was twelve. He's a good student and took everything in his stride, even Irish."

"The trouble started when he changed school?" I cut in.

"That's right. Not in school as such, but some of the students were involved in the attacks after school hours. That's why the school wouldn't help. It didn't happen on the premises. Nothing to do with them, they said."

"So how did it all start?"

"With the music. You heard Drago sing last night. He's very talented."

"That's putting it mildly," I said with feeling. "He'll be famous one day."

"I'm sure he will, if his voice holds after puberty. Anyway," Johnny continued, "as I said, it was Drago's singing that triggered the creeps to attack him. He won a talent competition and beat some of the top talents in the school, including the son of one of the local politicians."

"Let me guess," I interrupted. "Oliver O'Keefe's son?"

Johnny looked startled. "How did you guess?"

"Never mind. Go on."

"Okay. Well, after the competition, Drago was attacked by a gang of youths on his way home. In the park behind the supermarket. They didn't hurt him badly that time, just pushed him so he fell, and kicked him. But then someone came down the path, so they ran off."

"Did he see who they were?"

Johnny shook his head. "No. They wore hoodies and it was getting dark. He was pretty shaken, but we thought it was a one-off and it was probably some of the Travellers' kids having fun. We'd heard they did that sometimes for no reason. But we were wrong. It had nothing to do with the Travellers. It was a lot more serious than that."

"Did you report this to the Guards?"

Johnny sighed. "Yes. But they just took down some notes and we heard nothing. No evidence apart from Drago's bruises."

"And it happened again?"

Johnny's eyes hardened. "Yes. And there was stuff going on in school too. Drago's books were taken out of his locker and some of his homework that was in a folder. He got into trouble with the teachers, who accused him of lying when he said he couldn't find the work he'd done. Then the texts started arriving on his phone. Hateful things I wouldn't want anyone to see, names I wouldn't call anyone. We changed his number, but the attacks spread to Facebook and Instagram. Drago stopped using any social media. But we got slips of papers in the letter box. Then the final straw…Drago was attacked again."

"In the park?"

"No. At the bus stop one morning. He was on his way to a hurling match in Kilkenny, where the school was playing an away game. I've no idea how they knew he'd be there at that hour, all alone. But he was. They knocked him down so hard his arm was broken. They were wearing balaclavas, so he couldn't see their faces. But this time, he recognised a few of their voices. Two especially."

"Let me guess. One of them was the O'Keefe boy."

Johnny nodded. "And the other one is the son of an ex-Guard but now working in the county council. Says he's an independent like O'Keefe. But they're both very chummy with members of the Irish Democrats."

"I didn't know they had a contingent in Cloughmichael."

"They don't. But some quite prominent local people are members of the party. Don't laugh when I say this, but the Tidy Towns Committee is full of ID supporters."

I shook my head in disbelief. "Oh come on, Johnny. That's a little far-fetched."

"I swear. It makes me sad to be honest. Especially as it involves a friend of mine."

I stared at him. "A friend? Who? Not Fergal?"

"No. Not him."

"Who, then?" I said, willing him not to say the name that popped into my mind.

But he did.

CHAPTER 17

"Rory Quirke."

My heart sank. "What? No, that's not possible. Not Rory."

Johnny shrugged. "Afraid so. I was as surprised as you. Never thought he'd have anything to do with something so ultra-conservative and bigoted."

"Are you sure? I mean how do you know he's involved with them?"

"I saw him helping out at the church-gate collection for the party one Sunday. He stood there by that poster minding the collection pot, thanking everyone who contributed, and they all did. Everyone going into mass put something in. Some of them even saying stuff like 'good on ya'. I couldn't believe it. People going in to mass, for God's sake, and giving money to racists and actually applauding them. This is happening in my country in the twenty-first century." Johnny shook his head in disbelief.

"I know. It's awful. But going to mass every Sunday is not proof of true Christianity. But Rory…I can't believe he could possibly be active in this kind of group. There must be some explanation."

Johnny raised an eyebrow. "Why so shocked? Or are you disappointed? You don't fancy him, do you? And here I was, thinking you were more into Hollywood boys."

I suddenly didn't like Johnny as much as before. "What do you mean?" I demanded.

"We get the national newspapers here too. I happened to see that shot of you in a clinch with Colin Foley."

"What clinch? He grabbed me and kissed me on the cheek before I had time to pull away."

"It didn't look like you put up much of a fight to me."

"Oh please," I snapped. "You know how the media twist things."

"Yes, of course," Johnny said. "I know only too well."

I nodded. "Exactly. But enough about me. Let's look at the Irish Democrats. You seem to feel they're about to spread hatred all over this country. But that's your take. Maybe it isn't as bad as you make out? I've read that party is very conservative in their politics, but I haven't seen anything you could actually call racist or in any way neo-Nazi."

Johnny looked at me with a hint of pity. "You mean they're just a little old-fashioned?"

I took a sip of my coffee. "Weeell, um…" I tried to remember what the leader of that party had said the last time he stood up in the Dáil (Irish parliament). "They're very negative about asylum seekers and immigrants, of course. But so are a lot of people. Ireland isn't a wealthy country. The government's really stretching the budget to pay for health care and social housing, as well as taking care of refugees."

Johnny ate the last of his scone before he replied. "Kind of true. But look at the life these people left behind—if you can call it a life. If we raised taxes just a tiny bit, we could afford to be more generous. That's what the present government's trying to do, but that lot keep blocking them."

"O'Keefe is an independent," I cut in.

"Pfft," Johnny snorted. "Independent, my eye."

I gave up. Johnny was right. But I wasn't there to talk about that. "This isn't about politics," I argued. "Or about that political party. It's about those bullies and how to stop them."

"How are you going to do that? Don't tell me you're going to write about it in the Knockmealdown news."

"No. That would be stupid. There are other ways to deal with them. Better ways. Like turning the tide against them."

Johnny stared at me. "What are you talking about?"

I finished my coffee and pushed away the cup. "You'll see." I got up. "I'll be off now. Long drive back. I have a lot to consider. Thank you for talking to me."

Johnny got to his feet. "You're welcome. I just need your promise that you won't—"

"Don't worry. Sean Mac Aodhagáin's identity will not be revealed."

Johnny's shoulders relaxed. "Thank you."

"Except I have a feeling Drago's talent will be discovered one day. But by then everything will have sorted itself out and those bullies will have been disarmed and humiliated."

"Sounds impossible."

I winked. "Well, ya know, I do the hard things straight-away. The impossible takes a little longer."

He squeezed my hand in a warm handshake. "Good luck, Finola."

"Thanks. I'll need it."

I left the café and the quiet village, struggling with what Johnny had revealed. It couldn't be true. Rory involved with such a crowd? No, not possible. Or was it?

* * *

I arrived at the cottage late that night after a long drive through heavy traffic. I should have known Sunday evening after a beautiful weekend would be a bad time to take to those roads. But I just wanted to get home and crawl into bed, get a good night's sleep before I faced the naked truth about Rory and his political views. And then the task I'd set myself to fight the bullies. I'd been all gung-ho and bushy-tailed when I spoke to Johnny, but the reality wasn't as shiny as the dream. How on earth would I get started on my campaign? I needed to get the students in the school on my side before the leader of that gang got any whiff of what was going on. That was the answer. But the question was: how?

I pulled up outside the cottage as the setting sun dipped behind the mountains. I stopped for a moment and breathed in the soft air laden with the scent of grass and roses. Home. Was it? I nodded to myself. Yes, this was now home.

A movement beside the door made me jump. But it was only Jake, running up to greet me as if I'd been gone for months instead of just one day. I gathered him up in my arms, and he licked my face, whimpering and shivering with joy. I didn't notice the other shadow as I gave myself up to the pleasure of the reunion. But a touch on my shoulder made me jump and scream at the same time. Then I heard the voice and relaxed.

"Welcome back," Colin murmured in my ear.

I hit him a thump on the chest. "Shit, you scared me!"

"Sorry. Where have you been?"

"Away. What are you doing here so late?"

"Late? It's only ten o'clock. See? The sun's just set. I love these long northern evenings in Ireland."

I pulled back and looked at him. "You're still in costume."

"Yes. We just finished filming up at the house. I went down to see Jules, and she said you'd be home soon, so I decided to bring Jake to say welcome home." He did a little twirl to show off the wool pants, collarless shirt and knitted waistcoat. He lifted the tweed flat cap off his head "Evening, ma'am. This is what a young farmer would have worn in nineteen fifteen. Sexy, huh?"

"Not really," I said, thinking he'd be sexy in anything. I let Jake down. "But it's still late. I'm exhausted and I want to go to bed."

Colin threw away the cap and pulled me closer. "Me too. Yours."

"Don't be silly." I pulled away, trying to stop myself melting into his arms and whisper 'take me'. Sinking into bed with Colin would have been just what the doctor ordered. What was it about him that was so irresistible? His amazing good looks? The silky hair flopping over those green eyes? That deep voice in my ear? The hands on my waist? The smell of him? The feel of his body against mine? The—without thinking I grabbed hold of his face and kissed him hard on the mouth.

He laughed and put his arms around me and kissed me back. "That's what I meant," he mumbled against my mouth.

I couldn't help myself. I was too tired, too sad and far too attracted to this gorgeous man holding me—desiring me—to resist. And, God help me, I desired him right back. True love? Probably not, but definitely true lust. Whatever it was, it propelled us through the door and up the stairs to my little bedroom under the eaves, kissing, touching and removing clothes on our way. Jake tried to follow, but I broke away from Colin and gently lifted the dog into the kitchen and closed the door on his disappointed face.

By the time we stumbled into the bedroom, Colin had managed to remove all my clothes and expertly unclasped my bra and thrown it on the floor.

"Gee, you're good," I mumbled against his neck, pulling at the elastic of his boxers.

"I love your perfume," he whispered as we landed on the bed.

"It's not perfume, it's me," I whispered back.

"Even better."

I loved the smell of him, too: that mixture of aftershave, soap and just his skin, the way everyone has their own smell. Pheromones, I thought fleetingly as my body responded to his and we joined together in a crescendo of touching, kissing and moaning. I knew I was in the hands of an expert as I arched my hips to meet his erection. He made sure I was ready before he thrust into me—gently at first, with exquisite timing, until we reached the point of no return and the earth moved, the skies exploded in a riot of colours and sensations. The climax was the longest I'd ever experienced, and it slowly petered out, leaving me floating on a pink cloud of pure bliss.

I slowly opened my eyes and discovered Colin looking at me with such tenderness it nearly made me cry. I smiled and touched his face.

"You're amazing."

He took my hand and kissed it. "So are you. Or maybe *we* are? Together." He rolled off me.

I got off the bed and opened the door to the bathroom. "I'll be back in a minute."

He jumped up. "Let's shower together."

"We won't fit. The shower's tiny."

"Let's try anyway."

We did fit, even though it was a tight squeeze. We soaped up and then just stood there, our arms around each other while the warm water washed all the suds away.

"The water here feels lovely," Colin said. "So soft."

"It's wonderful." I closed my eyes and lifted my face to the warm gush from the shower.

Colin ran his hand over my wet hair. "Have you noticed how we're exactly the same height?"

"You're a little taller. I'm five nine. How about you?"

"Five eleven. But my publicist always puts six foot into any information."

"The water's cooling down. Let's dry ourselves and get into bed."

We squeezed out of the shower and dried each other. Then we got into bed, holding each other, whispering into the darkness, telling each other the stories of our lives. I told Colin about growing up in a family that barely held together, about my father's angry outbursts, about my brother and me hiding behind the sofa while Dad ranted on, shouting abuse at Mum. "Then I left. I just couldn't stand it anymore. I went to college and worked at all kinds of jobs to pay my way. My brother stayed behind, and when Dad died, he helped Mum get back on her feet and get a job. I always felt guilty about that."

"I don't think you need to feel guilty," Colin soothed. "You made your own way, paid for everything yourself. I'm sure your mum doesn't blame you."

"No. She's great. We get on quite well. But Seamus is her hero. Rightly so, of course."

"Sure."

I put my head on his shoulder. "Your turn."

"Okay. Not very exciting. Poor boy harbours dreams of acting. Gets job in factory and goes to acting classes in his spare time. Gets teased and bullied for being 'a fancy boy', a 'poofter' on housing estate. Then gets small part in TV series shot in County Cork, and the rest, as they say, is history."

"You were bullied?"

"Yeah," Colin said hoarsely. "Beaten up. Tarred and feathered—or the equivalent."

"I bet they're sorry now."

"Sorry in jail some of them. Most of them turned to crime. Horrible little shits, they were. But it takes a lot of hard work and determination to break out of an environment like that. I had the bug. None of them had any kind of dream." He turned and lay on his back, yawning. "Sorry love. My eyes are closing."

"Mine too."

Then we went to sleep under the blue duvet.

CHAPTER 18

The cock's crow woke me up. I blinked and looked around, but Colin was gone, along with his clothes. Jake lay yawning at my feet, and I thought for a second I'd dreamt it all. I stretched. What a dream. Colin and me—how crazy was that? Then I saw the cup of tea on the bedside table, with a rose placed beside it. The tea was still warm. He must have just left. I smiled. Typical. Tea and a rose but no note or even a text message. No promises, no declaration of love, no 'it was wonderful': just tea and a rose.

I drank the tea, smelt the rose, my mind lingering on the night before. It had come as no surprise that Colin was an amazing lover. But then he stepped out of the mould and shared some painful memories, things I'd never read about him or seen mentioned in interviews. And I'd revealed the uglier side of my own childhood. There was a bond between us—two Dubliners in an alien environment. Alien, because country life was so completely different from city living but also a cultural difference and that rough edge we acquired as children, growing up in the poorer part of a big city.

Colin now lived in LA, which had to be even more alien. Had it changed him? Had it made him cynical and hard? Was our night together just a brief fling? How did I feel about it? I asked myself. Did I want to get into something more permanent with Colin Foley? I laughed out loud. As if that was going to happen. He was just having fun. The sex had been outstanding and helped me out of the blue funk I was in. A lovely moment, that was all, leaving a lingering memory of something sweet. And so it should stay. Any thoughts of it being anything serious was ridiculous. I wasn't his type, and that was the understatement of the year.

"Stop dreaming, girl," I said to myself as I climbed out of bed. Jake jumped up and licked my face. I scooped him into my arms. He was the only male I could count on. It was time to get up, get dressed and get into gear.

* * *

The office was heaving with activity. Audrey and Dan were arguing about the photos he'd taken the day before, Audrey suggesting there should have been more close-ups of the main stars and not so many of the extras.

"What can I do when they beg me to take their pictures?" Dan demanded. "And the director isn't very cooperative when I want to take shots of the actors. Especially close-ups. 'we'll supply stills' he said."

"Stills," Audrey jeered. "How boring. We need candid shots of them being made up or getting into costume. Get that Caroline in curlers or something and Colin eating baked beans out of a tin. I've seen him do it when the catering staff were late with lunch." She tapped the photos laid out on the big table in the main office. "Some of these are fine, but we need more zip here, more candid-camera type of thing. It's all very well to print photos of the extras so they can show their mammies, but this is going out internationally. We need an *edge*, Dan."

"Yeah, right," he muttered.

Audrey sighed. "The elastic of your underpants works harder than you do."

Dan bristled. "Are you implying I'm fat?"

"No, honey," Audrey drawled. "I'm saying you're lazy."

I burst out laughing. "Gee, Audrey, you sure don't take any prisoners."

Audrey looked up. "I know, but this is important. Hi, Finola. How was your weekend break?"

"Lovely," I replied.

"Call for you," Sinead announced from the switchboard. "Rory Quirke."

I froze. "Tell him I'm not in."

"Um, I just told him you were here," Sinead replied.

I sighed. "I'll take it in my office."

"Hi," Rory said when I picked up. "How was the trip?"

"Great. Lovely part of Ireland."

"Yes." He paused. "So, did you find Johnny?"

"I did." I sank down on my chair.

"And? Did he tell you anything?"

"About what?" I said, trying to keep the dislike out of my voice.

"You know. Did he say anything about why he left or what happened before that?"

"Yes. But nothing you or I didn't know before. His son was continuously bullied and beaten up by a gang of youths. So they decided to go and live somewhere else. Can't say I blame them." I stood up and paced around my office. "I have to say it's pretty disgusting that this kind of thing goes on in Ireland in this day and age. I know this might be more blatant in this kind of area because of ignorance and a lack of sophistication. People around here live very narrow little lives and have narrow little minds. I found that in Ahakista, although it's so remote, people are a lot more tolerant and Christian than in this bigoted little bog town. Probably because there are so many foreigners and artists living there. In this town, people haven't moved for five hundred years. Who the fuck do they think they are?"

"Who are you talking about?"

"People living in small-town Ireland," I raged. "People who think less of others because they have darker skin and come from other countries. People who stand at church gates and collect money for Neo-Nazi parties before going inside to say prayers and give each other the sign of peace. How can they possibly live with themselves?"

Rory was silent for a long time, breathing heavily. "Who do you mean?" he whispered. "Me?"

"If the shoe fits." I slammed down the receiver. Then I kicked myself for letting rip like that. Maybe I should have been more diplomatic and not told him what I knew. But I lost it when I heard his voice and remembered what Johnny had said.

The phone rang again. I picked up on the first ring. "Rory, I didn't mean to imply—"

"It's not Rory. It's Aidan. Can I talk to you? You said I could call you—"

"Of course. Do you want to come to the office?"

"No, I can't right now. I have a maths class. But maybe you could come to my house at tea time? I'll be home around five."

"That'll be fine. I'll see you then, Aidan."

"Great. And…"

"Yes?"

"Don't tell anyone I called you."

* * *

Half an hour later, Rory burst into my office, his face red, his nostrils flaring. "What the hell did you mean by that?" he shouted.

I looked up from the computer screen. "Stop shouting. I think we need to talk."

"You're telling me."

"Sit down, please. I'm not going to talk to someone who looks like he's going to hit me."

Rory took a deep breath. "Right now, that's an option I'm seriously considering."

I picked up the phone. "Sinead. Call the Guards. I'm being threatened."

"Jesus!" Sinead breathed at the other end. "I thought he looked kind of weird."

Rory tore the receiver out of my hand. "Sinead, it's okay. I'm not going to hit anyone. We don't need the Guards."

"Sure?" I said.

"I swear."

"Cup of tea?" Sinead wheezed at her end.

"Perfect," I said and hung up.

Rory sat down, fished a crumpled hanky out of his pocket and wiped his face.

"You okay?" I asked.

"Fine," he muttered.

Sinead arrived with two mugs of tea and a packet of chocolate digestives on a tray, glancing nervously at Rory.

"You're an angel, Sinead," I said. "Nothing like a cup of tea to soothe the angry beasts."

She nodded. "It's Barry's tea too."

"Fabulous. It's okay. You can go back to the switchboard," I said, as Sinead hovered by the door. "I'll scream if he tries anything."

"I'll leave the door open," Sinead said and wobbled out of the room.

Rory folded his arms, glaring at me. "I'm waiting for an explanation."

I lifted an eyebrow. "How about you explaining to me about collecting money for that party outside the church gate? And you know what party I mean."

Rory looked confused. "I never—" Then he stopped.

"Oooh. Oookay...I know what you're talking about. That was an accident."

"An accident? Like you were hypnotised and forced to do it against your will? Pull the other one."

Rory made a pleading gesture. "Stop the sarcasm for a second and listen."

I grabbed one of the mugs and a biscuit and leaned back in my chair. "I'm all ears. This should be interesting."

Rory looked at his hands clasped around his mug of tea. "Okay. So this is what happened—it was my mother who was standing at the church gate, collecting for that party. She's a huge supporter of their politics. I'm not, and that's the truth. I hate what they stand for, hate that my mother supports them. We argue about that all the time. But that day, when I arrived at the church, my mother was suddenly taken ill. Someone helped her into the church, and I called an ambulance. While I waited, I stood beside the bucket with the money. I didn't really pay attention to it or the collection because I was worried about my mother. Then, the ambulance arrived, and I got into my car and followed. She was taken to hospital and treated for a minor heart attack. That was just after Christmas. I'd forgotten about the collection until you mentioned it."

"Oh. I see." I drank my tea and nibbled the biscuit. "You have a problem with your mother, my friend."

Rory sighed. "Yes. I do."

"She has a hold on you because of the farm."

"Big time." Rory sighed and looked up at me, his eyes full of pain. "I do love her in a way. And I understand how she feels about the farm and why she doesn't want to give it up. But I hate her political views. I think, though, she doesn't understand the implications. She thinks it's about the economy and about land. She just doesn't get the whole racist thing."

"Someone should enlighten her."

"Be my guest. Then you'll find out what it's actually like to talk to a wall." Rory's shoulders slumped even further.

I felt a pang of pity for this intelligent, attractive man, who, through no fault of his own, was so downtrodden by his mother. It was a huge dilemma. If he left the farm that was part of his very being, his life, his hopes, his very soul—he'd have been even more miserable. And that horrible woman knew it and used it. A Catch 22 situation. There had to be some solution, but no matter how I turned and twisted it, I couldn't find one.

"The wildlife sanctuary isn't going to happen either," Rory muttered and got up. "I have to go. Must check on the cattle and take care of a delivery."

I nodded, still deep in thought. The wildlife sanctuary… then I had a light-bulb moment. "Hey, Rory. Don't give up on that. I think I can help you."

"Yeah right," he scoffed. "So you think you can twist her arm?"

"No, but I think I…*we*…can shame her into it."

Rory stopped on the way to the door. "How?"

I smiled wickedly. "It's sneaky, but I know it'll work. This is what we're going to do…" I explained my idea to him in only a few words.

Rory's face brightened as he listened.

"Finola," he said, looking awestruck. "You're a sneaky bitch."

* * *

I penned a short article which I emailed to Audrey with a note, explaining what I wanted. There was just enough space to put this item on the front page of the Thursday edition if we moved the pony club competition and the charity walk to the second page. The pony-club mums would be ticked off, but it was a sacrifice that justified the means. Job done, I set off to my meeting with Aidan.

He was waiting for me in the unkempt garden, where he was gobbling up a mountain of sandwiches Miranda had just put in front of him. He looked up as I waded through the grass. I joined him and sat down on a rickety deckchair.

"Hi, Finola," he mumbled through his mouthful. "Just having a snack before supper."

I eyed the remains of the pile on the plate. "If that's a snack, I'd love to see what you eat for dinner."

"Two pounds of potatoes and half a chicken," Miranda said, as she made her way through the grass with a tray, her long skirt swishing around her legs. "Aidan has the appetite of an elephant. I brought you some tea and a ginger sponge I just took out of the oven."

"Lovely," I said as I eyed Aidan's skinny body, wondering where on earth he put it all. I sat back in the chair and looked around the garden with its gnarled apple trees, pink and yellow roses and the sweet peas with their heady scent. Despite the lack of care, this was an enchanting space, where butterflies flitted around and the sound of bees and birds soothed my overstressed brain. I closed my eyes and would have drifted off, if Aidan hadn't nudged my elbow.

I opened my eyes. "Sorry. I suddenly felt sleepy. It's such a peaceful garden." I looked around. "Where did Miranda go?"

"Back into the kitchen. She said she'd leave us to chat."

I sat up. "Okay, so let's chat. What was it you wanted to tell me?"

Aidan coughed. "Well, um…I had this idea. It might be stupid but I thought…"

"Come on, spit it out," I urged. "I could do with some ideas."

Aidan nodded. "Yeah, well, you see, I've been elected to the student council, and I also edit the school newspaper.

I read about that anti-bullying campaign in Sweden you mentioned. It's been very effective. So I thought we could do something similar. This way, no one's targeted directly, but if we can get enough students to join, we can set up a website and get someone to talk to us about bullying both in real life and on the Internet. I've already talked to the headmaster of our school, and he agreed that it was a very good idea. I think he knows very well who the bullies are, but he didn't want to go accusing anyone and stir up trouble." Aidan drew breath.

I looked at him with awe. "How old did you say you were?"

"Fourteen. Fifteen in August."

"Pity. Too young to run the government. But I'm sure it's written in the stars." I put my hand on his thin shoulder. "Aidan, you've just solved a huge problem. I'll work on an article about this, and we should also have a launch once it's all set up. We'll run it on Facebook and Twitter and everywhere we can. I want this to go viral."

Aidan blushed furiously. "Really? You like it?"

"Like it? I absolutely adore it."

"Oh, great. I had one more idea about how to make this really big."

"What's that?"

"I'd like you to ask Colin Foley if he'd endorse it. Would that be okay? I mean, you and he are…close…right?"

"We're friends, yes." Why did the mere mention of that name make me feel hot all over? I touched my cheek. Was I blushing? I got up to hide my discomfort. "I'll see if I can get a hold of him. Not a bad idea, though. Look, I have to go. And I'm sure you have homework to do."

"Yes, I do. Would it be okay if I started setting up the website? One of the guys in sixth year is really good at it. So it wouldn't cost anything."

"Of course. Set it up, and then I'll take look at it before

you publish. When do you think that bullying specialist will do his talk?"

"The headmaster said in a week or two. He wants to get it all going before the summer holidays."

"Good thinking. Bye for now, Aidan. See you soon."

"Bye, Finola. Thanks for coming. Let me know what Colin says."

"I will." I walked through the garden so deep in thought, I no longer paid attention to the birdsong or the humming of bees. How would I contact Colin after what had happened between us?

CHAPTER 19

The story was on the first page the following Thursday. Mary, the layout girl, had done a terrific job, putting a photo of Breda Quirke at the top, with the headline: **Breda Does Her Bit For Our Planet.** Then my name in the by-line and the short piece outlining Rory's plans for the wildlife sanctuary in detail, finishing with how all crop growers and fruit farmers in the area would be eternally grateful to Breda for sacrificing part of her land to make a better habitat for birds, bees and other wildlife, so essential for the growth of crops and for human survival. Pretty good article, I thought when I wrote it. Looking even better in print.

I had just finished reading it in my office, when Rory rang. "Great job, Finola. My mother's just seen it. She nearly had another heart attack."

"Is she okay?"

"Yeah. I thumped her on the back when she choked on her tea. She's fine. She was in the middle of an apoplectic rant to me when the phone rang. It was the local radio station asking if she'd agree to an interview."

"Bloody hell! What did she say?"

Rory laughed. "She was very gracious. Said she'd be happy to do it and then went on as if the wildlife sanctuary was her idea all along. She'll be on the afternoon show today. Then the phone rang again, and it hasn't stopped all morning. Everyone's congratulating her and saying she was a sly woman for keeping this secret. So she's still in the kitchen taking the credit. I had to leave, because I couldn't stop laughing. Brilliant move, Finola!"

"I know. It was one of those light-bulb moments. I knew we'd pull it off if we could find her weak spot."

"Yeah. And you did. Her vanity. She'll be insufferable after this. But it's worth it." He took a deep breath. "I owe you big time. How about dinner somewhere nice?"

"Sounds great. Where?"

"There's a lovely restaurant in Cashel, just opposite the Rock. Have you been there?"

"The Rock? I went there as a child, but I'd love to visit it again."

"Okay. Then we'll meet at the entrance. We could do the tour and then dinner?"

"Sounds terrific. Six o'clock?"

"Perfect." Rory said goodbye and hung up.

I stared at my phone as Audrey walked in. "What's the matter? Someone being rude to you?"

I shook my head. "No. But I accidentally agreed to go on a date with Rory Quirke."

She looked at me, confused. "But I thought you and Colin—?"

"No, that was just a story."

"Then going on a date with a nice-looking man like Rory should be something to look forward to, no?"

"No…I mean yes, of course," I replied, trying to get my emotions in line. "It's just to say thanks for the article, anyway. Breda Quirke is being hailed as the local queen of the environment after her fantastic initiative. She's basking in the glory of it all. She didn't even know she was doing it until she read it in the paper."

Audrey giggled. "I'd have loved to have seen her face when she saw it."

"She choked on her cup of Barry's. Rory had to do the Heimlich manoeuvre to save her. Then they rang from Tipp FM and asked for an interview. She couldn't very well say it was all lies and she had no interest in the environment."

"That's hilarious. Well done, Finola."

I shrugged. "Just one of those mad ideas that happened to work. So, how about you? Any mad ideas of your own?"

She sat down on the visitor's chair. "Not really. The new photos look good." She handed me a folder. "Take a look. There are some cute ones of Colin. Dan's new camera is really terrific. And he has a telephoto lens. The producer said we could go anywhere on the set as long as we were quiet during filming. I think we have nearly all we need."

"Oh, great." I opened the folder, flicking through the shots. "These are really good. Great detail. Very sharp, and—" My hand froze as I came to a shot of Colin and his co-star, Caroline O'Hara. "Oh my God," I whispered.

"What?" Audrey craned her neck. "I haven't seen them all. What's that one?"

I held it up for her to see. "They seem to have made friends at last."

"Oops. I'm not sure that's going to be in the movie. Are they in costume? I can't see."

"Not exactly," I remarked, pushing the photo behind the others. "It looks like they're very much out of their costumes."

Audrey reached for the pile of photos and pulled out the last one. "I have a feeling Danny boy got a little trigger happy with the telephoto lens. They appear to be in someone's trailer here. Probably hers."

"Tear it up," I ordered. "And tell Dan to delete it from his file."

"Okay." There must have been something in my voice that made Audrey obey instantly. She tore the photo into tiny pieces and threw it into my waste paper bin. "There."

I fixed her with my gaze. "We didn't see it, right?"

Audrey looked at me blankly. "See what?"

"I have no idea." I looked through the rest of the photos. They were all excellent, and this time, Dan had made an effort and got some great close-up shots of the cast and crew in all kinds of situations. "All brilliant," I said. "And I love the light and the great backgrounds. Full marks to you and Dan."

"I knew once I lit a fire under him, he'd get going."

"No better woman to do it. Can I leave it up to you to pick out the best ones? Show me what kind of layout you're planning. Then we'll send it to the marketing team and get their approval, and we're away."

Audrey nodded and got up. "They want us to release the magazine in a couple of weeks, when the filming here is over. There'll be some kind of cast party we've all been invited to, so we could combine it with the launch of the magazine."

"A couple of weeks? You mean they'll leave then?"

"Yup," Audrey said from the door. "They're going to shoot some interiors in Dublin and then the rest in LA."

"I see."

"I'll get going on this, so," Audrey said and closed the door, leaving me deep in thought, trying to sort out my feelings about those candid shots I'd seen. Colin and Caroline O'Hara in her trailer, practically naked. Snogging, like randy teenagers.

* * *

The Rock of Cashel, a spectacular group of medieval buildings set on an outcrop of limestone above the town with the same name, was bathed in the mellow evening sunlight. According to the brochure I was handed at the gate, the round tower was from the twelfth century, and the high cross and cathedral were built only a few years later. I'm not a huge history buff or into sightseeing, but this place had a kind of magic I couldn't resist. I could feel the wings of ancient history as I looked up at the towers and crenulations, made by many hands a thousand and more years earlier. What a forbidding place this must have been, still quite beautiful in a stark, spiritual way. And those monks, living, toiling, reading and creating the beautiful handcrafted manuscripts that still exist today.

Lost in thought, I jumped as someone called my name. I turned and discovered Rory coming up the hill.

"Hi, there," I called. "Why aren't you dressed in monk's clothing?"

"Too hot. I like your dress."

"Thank you. It was too warm to wear jeans and this was all I had. A summer dress I bought in Boston when I was working on my book." I rubbed my bare arms, feeling slightly self-conscious. I hardly ever wore skirts or dresses. But it was such a warm evening with the heat of the day still lingering in the soft wind. I'd pulled out the simple summer dress, put it on and done a twirl in front of the mirror. My arms and legs were pale, but in good shape, so why not?

Rory drew closer. "You must tell me about your time in Boston one day."

"I will. One day," I said airily, knowing I probably wouldn't. The time in Boston and my brief relationship with Cory, with whom I'd worked on my book, was a memory laced with pain and disappointment. Not a place I wanted to revisit. The past was the past.

Rory smiled at me as he arrived at my side. "Did you listen to the interview?"

I laughed. "Yes. Must say Breda knows how to work the media. I had no idea she was such a ham. 'I'm considering keeping bees. And then I could produce honey. Much healthier than marmalade or jam,'" I mimicked in Breda's deep voice. "She didn't once mention that it was all your idea."

Rory shrugged. "Who cares? At least we're doing it. She's already booked contractors to prepare the fields. Then we'll be planting in September. I'm really happy about that, you know."

"You must be. And I'm pleased for you. So…let's go and see this rock then."

"Yes, we'd better hurry. They're closed to the public after five, but I managed to get them to let us in so we can roam around on our own."

"That's grand. I don't really like guided tours. I prefer silence so I can get the vibes of times past."

"Me too."

We didn't talk much as we entered the monastery, each lost in our own thoughts. We wandered around the ruins and walked into the cathedral, its ancient stone walls surrounding us as we looked up at the vaulted ceiling and the recently restored frescoes in the Vicar's Choral, where the laymen appointed to chant during the services would have sat. I could nearly hear the many voices chanting as I stood there, and a chill crept over me that had nothing to do with the temperature.

I walked out and went to the edge of the rock, looking out over the valley. Blue-grey clouds gathered on the horizon, and there was a roll of distant thunder. Such a dramatic backdrop to this ancient site, where the kings of Munster would have reigned many years before Christianity began.

Rory joined me and stood there without speaking, looking out at the green fields and rolling hills beyond. I suddenly realised how much he was part of this land, this earth, as his ancestors would have been here even before the Rock was built.

"Magic," I breathed.

"So timeless."

"Eerie."

He touched my arm. "And now I'm hungry. Come on, let's eat."

I pulled out of my daydream and left the ancient kings to their rock. We walked back down the hill and across the street to a quaint restaurant called Chez Hans, situated in a converted chapel. There was no end to the religious vibes in this town.

"It was a Protestant chapel until the nineteen fifties," Rory informed me as we were guided to a round table near what would have been the altar.

There was still a chapel feel to the room, with its high vaulted ceiling, beams and stained-glass windows. But there was nothing religious about the guests, whose jolly chatter and laughter echoed around the restaurant. I was a little disappointed that Rory had chosen a restaurant with this kind of busy, cheery feel, rather than something candle-lit and intimate. I expected him to make romantic overtures, which I'd have welcomed after the revelations about Colin and his co-star. There's nothing like a little flirting to make a jilted woman feel better. And in any case, I was beginning to feel Rory and I were compatible. He was good-looking, intelligent and fun. What's not to like? I said to myself as we studied the menu in companionable silence.

We'd just ordered the starter and main course—heirloom salad for me (just to stay with the historical theme), smoked salmon for him, followed by fillet steak with celeriac purée for us both, as we agreed we were starving after all the sightseeing and climbing around in ruins—when two very familiar people walked in. I blinked and stared. Caroline O'Hara and Colin. They were shown to a table at the back of the room, away from the most popular tables.

Colin looked straight at me as he sat down and nodded in a way that simply said, "I've seen you." Then he turned his attention to Caroline, who looked devastating in a tight black dress and a necklace with multi-coloured beads.

I suddenly sprang into action. I'd never used this clichéd way of making a man jealous—I've never had to, but without thinking, I turned to Rory and beamed him a smile. Then I took his hand and leaned over and planted a kiss on his cheek.

He pulled back, smiling. "What was that for?"

"For taking me out to dinner." I knew he couldn't see the couple, as he was sitting opposite me. But I had a full frontal view, and they looked very cosy indeed.

Rory looked confused. "But that was to thank *you*. You don't owe me any gratitude."

I kept smiling sweetly. "I was just feeling so good, and that's your doing."

"Oh. Well, in that case, I'm happy." He took my hand and gave it a little squeeze. "But maybe we shouldn't look too… er, friendly?"

"Why not?"

Rory coloured slightly. Then, still holding onto my hand, he started to talk in a voice so low, I had to lean in even closer to hear him. "It doesn't take much around here to start the gossip. And once it starts, it's impossible to stop."

"I don't care. Do you?"

Rory looked at me as if he was trying to make a decision. "I have something to tell you," he mumbled conspiratorially. "It's highly confidential, so I need you to promise first that you won't tell anyone about this."

I nodded, startled by the intensity in his voice and eyes. "Of course. I swear."

Rory nodded and leaned closer still. "It's about a woman—a girl I loved very much."

I swallowed and pulled my hand out of his. "I see. Go on."

"She lives in Dublin and she's an archaeologist. She's worked on a number of high-profile digs all over Ireland."

"Sounds great," I mumbled. "So where's the problem? Wouldn't your mother have been over the moon if you married her?"

"No. She would have been spitting nails and would have disinherited me."

I stared at Rory. "Why? What was the problem?"

"Anita—that's her name—isn't Irish. She's originally from Iraq…and a Muslim."

I blinked. "Oh. Christ, yes. I see. That wouldn't have gone down well with Breda."

Rory's laugh was bitter. "Are you kidding?"

I forgot all about Colin and Caroline. "So what happened?"

Rory looked up as our starters arrived and busied himself with squeezing lemon on his smoked salmon. "First of all, I should explain that Anita's an Irish citizen. She came here with her parents when she was ten. She was a top student and speaks fluent Gaelic." Rory met my gaze. "She isn't a practising Muslim, doesn't wear the hijab or anything. In fact, she's broken away from her parents, and that wasn't easy. She's now actively campaigning for women's rights."

"Good for her."

Rory nodded. "She's very strong. We need women like her in this country. Why can't people see that?"

I put my hand on his arm. "I certainly can."

He nodded. "Yes, *you* can, but try to convince the old Ireland."

"And Breda. Old Ireland personified," I muttered.

"You're telling me."

"What about her? Anita? How did she feel about you and the farm and the way you're so rooted to it?"

Rory sighed and looked morosely at his plate. "She understood completely but not that I can't stand up to my mother. After all, she broke away from her own parents and defied everything they held dear. So why couldn't I do the same?"

"You would if it was only about religion and tradition," I argued. "But in your case, it's about your inheritance, the right to own your family property and land. You can't give that up even for true love. If you did, I imagine it would cause problems later on in a marriage."

Rory nodded. "Yes, it would. And she couldn't understand that. I invited her down here for a weekend to show her the farm and tell her how we've been here since time began. She stayed at the Bianconi Inn. I took her for a tour of the farm, and I introduced her to my mother."

"You did?" I stared at him in astonishment. "What happened? I bet it wasn't a lovely get-to-know-you around the tea and scones."

Rory let out a bitter little laugh. "It certainly wasn't. The atmosphere was chilly, to say the least. Polite conversation laced with venom from both sides. And Mam kept asking stupid question about Iraq and 'your religion', as she put it. She even asked why Anita wasn't wearing 'one of them veils'. I thought I was going to die of shame. Then Anita got up and walked out without saying goodbye, and I had to run after her to take her to the train. She told me never to come near her again. Or at least not until I told my mother to move out. Which is the same as never, of course." Rory sighed and poked at his food with his fork. "She called me a wimp."

"That's a bit harsh. But true, I'm afraid." I felt a surge of anger as I said it. Yes, he was a bit of a wimp. He'd also misled me, making me think he was interested in me while he was still pining for another woman.

"Gee, thanks." He shrugged. "But what else would you say?"

The fillet steaks arrived, smelling mouth-wateringly good. I picked up my knife and fork. "Let's not waste this amazing food by arguing."

"Right." Rory brightened and attacked his steak with gusto, and we ate in silence, while I shot a glance at Colin and his date. They were looking at a piece of paper and talking in a low voice, their heads together. The steak suddenly felt like a lump of cardboard in my mouth.

Rory finished eating and put his cutlery down with a clatter. "I'm going to do it," he declared.

I swallowed and pulled my attention away from the couple behind him. "Do what?"

"Tell her. Breda. My mother. Things will be done my way, or I'll leave. I can't stand this anymore, and I'm really sorry, Finola."

"Sorry? For what?"

"For throwing all my problems at you and for maybe making you believe I was attracted to you. I was *trying* to fall for you so that I'd forget about Anita, and then you and I could—" He stopped, looking embarrassed. "Not that I didn't find you attractive, of course. I certainly did—do. What man wouldn't? But…"

I rolled my eyes. "How old are you? Twelve? Please, grow up, will ya."

He sighed and pushed away his plate. "I know. You're right. I should stop dreaming and decide what to do. It's not fair to anyone—even my mother."

"You bet it isn't. Not even fair to me."

"No. That's why I said sorry. I hope you weren't falling—" He stopped and laughed. "Of course not. You're not the romantic type, are you?"

I glared at him. "And why wouldn't I be? Okay, so I haven't had much luck in the romance department, but that doesn't mean I'm not romantic." I leant forward and fixed him with my gaze. "I was kind of attracted to you for about ten seconds, Rory," I said softly. "And who knows where that might have led? But I've been through two botched engagements, so I suppose that makes me a little wary."

"I can imagine. I'm sorry if I—"

"Please, forget it. Let's just be friends. No commitment or demands or any of that shit."

Rory relaxed. "Sounds good to me. Do you want dessert?"

"No thanks. Could we leave now?" I suddenly didn't want to sit there anymore and listen to Rory's woes while watching Colin get up close and personal with Caroline. I

The Blow-In

could see out of the corner of my eye that he had his hand on her knee. He glanced at me, winked and then turned his attention back to her. Conceited shit. Feeling up one woman while winking at another. Typical.

Rory paid the bill and we left. I swished past Colin's table, pretending not have seen him, but he grabbed my arm and stopped me.

He got to his feet. "Hi, Finola."

"Oh, hi, Colin," I said with fake surprise. "Didn't see you there in the dark." I squinted at Caroline who was looking at me with ill-disguised venom. "Caroline O'Hara?" I held out my hand and shook hers that felt like a cold dead fish. "Hi. I'm Finola. Don't think we've met. I run the local paper in Cloughmichael."

"I've heard of you," Caroline said. "Nice to meet you."

"Lovely," I gushed. "I'd stay to chat but we have to go."

Caroline smiled stiffly. "Pity. Catch up with you another time, perhaps?"

"Yes," I purred. "Let's do lunch." I wiggled my fingers at them. "Bye for now. See you around, Colin." I followed Rory out the door before Colin had a chance to reply.

I had to stop for moment outside to pull myself together. Rory was further down the street, looking morosely into the distance. What an evening. The best part had been the visit to the Rock. It had been downhill all the way since then.

Rory turned and looked at me. "Will I see you to your car?"

"I'm parked just below the entrance to the monastery. Where's yours?"

He pointed at his jeep further down the street. "Just there."

"Maybe you should get going then. There's no need for you to escort me."

"Are you sure?"

"Positive. Thanks for a lovely evening. Let me know how it goes with your mum and the farm."

He kissed my cheek. "Thanks for listening."

"You're welcome." I patted him on the arm. "Bye for now, Rory."

"Bye, Finola."

I watched him drive off. Another potential romance had bitten the dust.

CHAPTER 20

"What's wrong with me?"

Jules studied me for a moment. "In what way? I don't see anything wrong with you except your hair needs a cut and you look very down."

We were in Jules's messy, cosy sunroom enjoying a glass of wine after I'd burst in on her on the way home from my date with Rory.

I ran a hand through my hair. "I know. I should shave my head or something. Get a few tattoos, maybe, just to change my whole look?"

Julie topped up my glass. "Are you mad? Don't change anything. Just get it cut shorter and put in some more of those funky purple highlights. I loved that."

"Yes. Maybe." I looked morosely out the window into the old orchard, where, in the gathering dusk, Jake was fooling around with Jules's dogs, having a great time fighting over an old shoe. I looked back at Jules, reclining on the couch, a cushion behind her head. "Thanks for not asking how the date went."

"I guessed it probably wasn't a huge success."

"Ha." I snorted. "That's putting it mildly. It was a roaring disaster. There I was, tossing my hair and winking at Rory, and he didn't even notice. I have a feeling he thought I was just being friendly because my attempt at flirting opened up the floodgates, and he started telling me about some woman he's been unhappily in love with. But then, just to make everything even more wonderful, in walks Colin with that Caroline woman and they immediately start practically snogging right in front of me."

Jules lifted an eyebrow. "Snogging? At Chez Hans? That must have stirred up that stuffy place."

"Well, not exactly snogging, but there were hot vibes. He even had his hand on her leg under the table."

"Bloody hell. What a cheeky bastard."

"Yeah, he is."

Jules leaned forward. "But you're hot for him, aren't you?"

"Yeah," I said glumly. "You got it in one."

"I bet he fancies you too."

"Funny way of showing it."

"He's trying to make you jealous, I bet."

I shrugged. "I bet he isn't. He's just the kind of guy for whom having sex is just a recreation."

"What?" Jules sat up. "You had *sex* with Colin Foley? Holy shit! And you never told me. When did this happen? Was it fabulous?"

I wound my legs around each other and put the glass on the small table beside my chair. "Shit, I shouldn't have told you. But okay. It happened last week when I came back from West Cork. He just appeared at my door. I was tired and emotional. I wasn't thinking straight. I just grabbed him and started kissing him and then, well…you know. And yes, it was incredible. That's all I'm going to say."

Jules stared at me with awe. "Wow. *You* grabbed *him*?"

"Oh, please. Shut up. I don't want to talk about it. I've said too much already. Can we forget it?"

"How on earth could I forget that? Can you?"

"No."

Jules sighed. "Neither could I if it happened to me. So then he just left right afterwards?"

"No, he stayed all night. He was gone when I woke up, but he left a cup of tea and a rose on my bedside table." My eyes filled with tears. I dashed them away, hoping Jules wouldn't notice.

"How sweet."

"Yeah, and then he goes and sleeps with his co-star and snogs her in public for all to see. Such a darling, isn't he?"

"You don't know he was sleeping with her. Maybe he wasn't?"

"I know for a fact that he did." I sighed and picked up my glass again. "Can we talk about something else?"

"But this was getting interesting," Jules complained. "I don't have a love life, so I have to live vicariously through you."

"Then you'll be extremely bored, my friend." I yawned and joined her on the sofa. "I'm exhausted after all this. Can I sleep here tonight?"

Jules got up. "Of course. I'll just let the dogs in. Jake can sleep in here with you." She threw a blanket at me. "Here, pull this over you and lie down."

I was going to laugh and tell her I was only joking but suddenly felt unable to move. I snuggled under the blanket, and after Jake had joined me and settled on my feet, I closed my eyes and drifted off.

* * *

I went back to the cottage to shower and change the next morning and found several email messages when I switched on my laptop. The first one was from Aidan:

Hi, Finola,

Just to let you know that the website's up and running (only the first page, more to come), the link is below. We're going to have a link to the Swedish website and the English version of their course for parents on how to tackle bullying of younger children. Then we're setting up a helpline in the form of a forum that we'll moderate very carefully. Unfortunately, the psychologist let us down, but we're planning to get someone in the music business to come and speak to the students on the day of the launch, which will be even better. If you could write something about this in the paper, that would be terrific. See you soon,

Cheers,
Aidan.

I clicked on the link and a website with clear and concise texts and graphics came into view. It would be very easy to navigate once all the relevant pages were up.

Impressive. These guys were more clued up than middle-aged politicians. I suddenly felt old and behind the times. I got ready and went to the office, where I immediately started work on the piece about the new campaign. The launch would be at the school on Friday night, and I had to make it catchy and stress how important this new move was and how we all had to support it. I asked Audrey to contact the radio station and looked up the number to the constituency offices of the major political parties. I was sure they'd all come. Great chance to look good for all of them.

Audrey arrived, breathless, a little later. "Great news," she announced. "The school kids got someone really famous to talk at their launch on Friday. This is going to be hot!"

I didn't look up from my article. "Who did they get?" I asked, as I skimmed through the text, trying to catch typos.

"Colin Foley."

My hand froze and my jaw dropped. "What? Are you sure?"

"Positive." Audrey winked. "I'd say his publicist put him up to it. Great chance of mega kudos, ya know."

"Lots of emails," Sinead shouted from her desk. "The county council will be there and the local politicians too, including our TD. Plus..." she paused for breath, "national television is sending a crew."

"RTE?" I shouted back.

"They're the guys, yes," she shouted back.

"Jesus," Audrey whispered. "What'll I wear?"

"I'm sure you'll think of something," I replied, wondering the same thing myself.

* * *

Audrey wore her trademark micro-mini skirt and thigh-high boots, her hair in an elaborate chignon and a ton of make-up. "In case there'll be a close-up," she whispered as I joined her at the back of the hall on the night of the launch. I was in the dress I wore at the Rock and had my hair cut very short at a hairdresser's in Clonmel called Curl up and Dye. I chickened out at the dyeing stage, worried it might turn out really weird.

"Maybe later?" I promised and raced back home to stick my head under the shower to get most of the hairspray out.

When I walked into the packed school hall, I wondered how Audrey could possibly think the cameras would be pointed at her. I looked at the stage, where Colin was talking to the headmaster and testing the mike. He looked amazing in a tight tee shirt, skinny jeans and sneakers, his hair gelled. Even from my vantage point at the back, I saw his green eyes sparkle in the spotlights and his teeth gleam against his light tan. I realised then what true star quality was, and he had it in spades. But it wasn't until he started speaking and his deep voice rang out in the silent hall that the full power of his charisma was released. There must have been five hundred people there, mostly students, but he still managed to keep them enthralled, not so much with his voice but with what he said.

Colin pulled no punches. He got straight to the point, first revealing details of his own childhood and how he'd been bullied and attacked for being different. Then he went on to condemn bullies in general, calling them slime and cowardly gobshites. His eyes blazed, his fists clenched, and his face contorted in anger as he talked. There was no doubt about his passion for this cause. I had a feeling that everyone present held their breath during Colin's diatribe. There was a long silence when he finished, and then the hall erupted in ear-splitting shouts, whistles and applause that lasted a good ten minutes.

Colin held up a hand and waited for silence. "Okay," he said when the noise abated. "That was me. But how about you? How many of you have been bullied or at least intimidated recently? By that I mean little insults that grow to being pushed around and even attacked. Or having hateful text messages sent to your phone or comments on Facebook." He looked across the audience. Two hands shot up, then another two and then more and more.

Colin nodded. "Yeah, I see it's quite common. And I bet those of you who have been bullied like that are perhaps a little different. Maybe you're from another country, or your parents are, or you're the youngest in the class, or you wear glasses or any other thing that makes you stick out as vulnerable. Am I right?"

Nods and murmurs among the kids in the audience. Colin had hit the nail on the head there.

"I see there are quite a few here. But what do we do about it?" he asked. "How do we deal with these cowardly shits who hide behind pseudonyms? We can't make them stop. They'll only take on another fake name and start again. They do it for kicks and to have power over those they deem weaker than them. I'm no expert in dealing with bullies, but I know you must never let them win or obey when they threaten you with violence if you tell anyone." Colin raised his voice to a near shout. "If you're bullied, go and tell an adult, a parent or a teacher. Never, ever allow these creeps to escape. That's all I can tell you right now. But the fantastic website that Aidan Murphy and his friends have put together also has a lot of tips and a help page. It's one of the most brilliant sites I've ever seen. Use it. Support it. Spread the word about it wherever you can." He waved a clenched fist. "Bullies out there, be afraid. Be very afraid!"

More applause and shouting. The flashing of cameras and lights was nearly blinding. Then the headmaster took the mike, clapped Colin on the back and made his own little speech, endorsing what Colin had just said, inviting all present politicians up on the stage.

Then Colin grabbed the mike back and shouted, "Aidan Murphy! Come on the stage, please."

There was a movement in the crowd as Aidan pushed through to the stage, blushing furiously. When he was finally up there by Colin's side, the headmaster asked him to say a few words.

Aidan, blushing even more, took the mike. "Thank you for the support, guys," he mumbled into the mike. "I should thank Eamon Sullivan for setting up the website and for doing all the links to the Swedish one. We're hoping to spread the word across Europe. But most of all, I want to thank Finola McGee for helping me understand how important this is. If it wasn't for her, we wouldn't be here doing this today." His eyes scanned the crowd. "If you're here, Finola, please come and say a few words."

"Oh, no," I muttered and sidled to the door. Not me on that stage, no way. Audrey pulled at me, but I tore away and got out before anyone could invite me to come forward. I could still hear shouting and whistling as I walked down the street to my car. I knew I was being a chicken, but I couldn't face standing in the limelight with Colin and getting some kind of accolade I didn't deserve. It was Aidan's night, and no way did I want to steal his thunder. Nor did I want to have Colin fake some kind of affection for me, and that was my greatest fear now that I knew the truth about him and his co-star.

"Miserable shit," I said as I drove home, just to make myself feel better. Of course he wasn't a shit or miserable. His fooling around with me and my feelings had nothing to do with the magnificent performance I'd just witnessed. And the trouble was, it made me love him more.

Love? How did that thought enter my head? Did I love Colin? I slowed the car as I came to the gates of Jules's farm, and came to a stop. I stared out into the darkness and finally allowed myself to relax and admit that yes, I did love him. Not that it made me happy; it just had a calming effect to have finally realised it. I started the car again and drove on, ignoring my phone beeping with a message. Probably Audrey telling me to go back. I'd go to the office later to write up a piece about the event and get all the photos so they could be included. I needed a short break before I headed into the office to catch my breath and watch the report of the event on TV.

I parked, grabbed my bag and phone and went inside to turn on the evening news. It would be good to see how it all looked from the outside.

I settled on the sofa with Jake on my lap and turned on the small TV set. After the main headlines, the anti-bullying campaign was the major news item. Colin and the headmaster came onto the screen, and then I could watch Colin's incredible delivery up close. He was even more impressive on TV.

Then they came to Aidan's little speech and his request for me to talk. The camera scanned the crowd, but instead of me, Audrey pushed through and climbed up on the stage, helped by a clearly delighted Colin, who got an eyeful of her slim thighs before she stood at his side, talking into the mike as if she had done nothing else her whole life.

"Hello, my name is Audrey Killian," she said in her husky voice. "Unfortunately, Finola had to rush to an important meeting, so I'll talk on her behalf. Finola has always hated bullying of any kind, as indeed we all do. She knew that something like this was going on in the town and that it was escalating. Indeed, rumour has it that some families have had to move from here to escape the bullying, both verbal and physical, their children have had to endure." There was a communal gasp, followed by murmur in the audience.

Audrey pressed on. "Then Finola had a chat with some young people in the area, and this gave them the push to take this initiative. Aidan had the brilliant idea of a website after reading about the Swedish campaign, and now I think it will snowball into something huge that will help stamp out bullying. So here's to Finola, who got the ball rolling. Let's give her a big clap."

The crowd erupted into clapping, cheering and shouts of 'Finola!' I couldn't help feeling moved and my eyes welled up. What a sweet girl Audrey was. I flicked on my phone, deciding to check my message and reply to her text.

It wasn't from Audrey. It was from Colin. *Where did u go? We wanted to cheer for u. Party at the Inn. Please come back and join the fun. Not for me, but for Aidan. C x*

X? As in kiss? That was the part of the message that made my stupid heart flip. It took me two seconds to decide what to do. I put Jake in the kitchen and closed the door on his sad little face, got into the car and headed back to town. And the Inn.

CHAPTER 21

I found the candlelit bar at the Bianconi Inn deserted. Confused, I looked around, wondering if I'd misunderstood Colin's message. He said there was a party, but there wasn't even a waiter around. The piped music played Sinatra songs and the candles flickered, throwing pools of light on the mahogany tables scattered around the room. I walked across the plush carpet and peered across the bar counter, but there was no one to even serve a drink.

Was this some kind of silly joke? Annoyed, I decided to go to the office. I didn't have time to play games. But before I reached the door, a waiter appeared, carrying a bottle of champagne in a cooler and some glasses. He placed them on one of the tables.

He looked at me. "Miss McGee?"

"Yes?"

"Mr Foley said to expect you. May I serve you a glass of champagne?"

"Yes," I replied. "Fine. Thanks. But I was expecting a party. Where is everybody?"

He looked confused. "Party? No, there's no party here, as far as I know. Mr Foley and his guests will be with you shortly." He expertly popped open the bottle, poured me a glass and handed it to me. Then he nodded and disappeared behind the counter. I sat down and sipped the champagne, thinking I'd leave once I'd finished the glass. What the hell was Colin up to?

I was sitting there, fuming about having been brought into town on false pretences, when Colin, Jerry, Miranda and Aiden walked in.

I got up and greeted Miranda and Jerry with a kiss on the cheek and clapped Aiden on the back, trying not to meet Colin's eyes.

"Hi there," I said. "I was wondering what was going on."

Colin grabbed my elbow and planted a light kiss on my cheek. "It got too noisy in the pub, and in any case, Aidan's under age, so he couldn't even be there. Here at the Inn there are different rules, especially if you're an invited guest."

I pulled away. "I see." I swallowed and composed myself, smiling at Aidan. "Congratulations, Aidan. It was a great presentation. Sorry about bailing out, but I felt it was your evening."

Aidan nodded. "Yeah, that's okay. I understand why you didn't want to be up there with the lights and the cameras and TV and everything. I thought it was pretty cool, though," he added and blushed.

"Totally cool," I agreed. "I could tell you liked the buzz too."

Aidan laughed. "Yeah, I did. Some of the girls who were there asked for my autograph, and several of them wanted me to pose with them in their selfies."

"I think you created a monster, Finola," Jerry remarked.

"And Colin had huge competition tonight," Miranda added. "Nobody even looked at him."

Colin laughed. "Yes, I feel really old now." He went to the bar counter. "Hey, Fintan, could you pour my guests some champagne?"

The waiter reappeared. "Of course, Mr Foley. I was just telling the girls in the kitchen to bring out some snacks."

Colin nodded. "Perfect. So why don't we sit down and enjoy a little bit of bubbly and some finger food?"

We all sat down around a table and drank champagne and nibbled on cocktail sausages and tiny sandwiches. I realised how hungry I was and wolfed down the food on my plate in seconds.

"Sorry. I forgot to have dinner," I said when I noticed everyone looking at me.

Miranda handed me a plate of sausage rolls. "Here. There's more than enough for us all." She stood up. "We have to go in any case."

"But it's not that late," Colin protested. "Only nine o'clock."

"I know, but the boys have homework," Miranda replied. She ruffled Aidan's hair. "And you have a maths test tomorrow. So come on, rock star, you have to make sure you get through school before you can get back into the limelight."

Jerry and Aidan joined Miranda, said their goodbyes and before I had time to move, left me all alone with Colin. And a plate of sausage rolls. I looked at the plate and felt Colin's eyes on me.

"Are you going to eat all that?" he asked, his voice full of laughter.

I put the plate on the table. "No. I've suddenly lost my appetite."

He lifted the bottle. "More champagne? This bottle's empty, but I can order some more."

I got up. "No, I have to work later. Not to mention drive home."

"You could always stay here, of course."

I met his eyes. The invitation I saw there made my face hot. "No thanks."

Colin stood up and took my hand. "I want to tell you something."

I pulled away and picked up my bag. "Yeah, I'm sure you do. But whatever it is, I don't want to hear it."

He put up his hands in a gesture of surrender and backed away. "Okay, if that's what you want. I thought we had something pretty special, but that was probably just me being foolish."

I stopped on the way to the door. "Something special?" I spat. "Is that what you have with Caroline too?" I turned away to hide the tears welling up, fumbling with the door handle, but Colin leapt across the room and stopped me.

"What are you talking about?" he asked. "Caroline and me—that's impossible. I thought you knew that."

I stared at him. "Knew what?"

Colin sighed and let his arms fall. "Caroline's gay, you eejit."

My breath caught in my throat. "What? She's gay? I didn't know that. I thought she was married?"

Colin nodded. "Yes. She is. To a woman. They got married shortly after gay marriage was made legal in Ireland. But it wasn't reported in the press then, because she wasn't that well known. She still isn't, but that'll change when the movie comes out."

"Oh." I paused while I tried to digest this latest piece of information. "But what about you and her and that dinner date? I saw you put your hand on her leg and wink at me at the same time. What the hell was that?"

Colin rolled his eyes. "I thought you'd get it. It was supposed to be a little joke between you and me. I was sure you knew about Caroline."

"How would I know? I haven't had much contact with her, as she's been locked up in her trailer most of the time, doing her great Garbo-I-want-to-be-alone act.'"

Colin shrugged. "Yeah, I know. But you're a bloody journalist, aren't you?"

I folded my arms. "A journalist, yes. But I can't actually read minds, you know." Something that had been niggling me popped into my mind. "Okay, if Caroline's gay, as in preferring women to men, what about that night in her trailer. You and her—naked, involved in some rather intimate… stuff," I ended lamely.

Colin stared at me. "What? In her trailer..." He frowned. "How did you know about..."

I sighed. "I'm afraid Dan got a little too enthusiastic about taking pictures with his new camera. He must have pointed his telephoto lens in the wrong direction."

"Jesus, that's awful," Colin exclaimed. "I see you might have come to all the wrong conclusions if you saw that. But believe me, nothing happened. It wasn't even in her trailer—it was in mine. We were rehearsing the pivotal love scene of the movie." Colin ran his hand through his hair. "So Danny boy must have caught that with his new toy. But there was nothing remotely sexy going on, I swear."

I lifted an eyebrow. "Really? That's not what it looked like to me."

Colin put his hands on my shoulders and stared into my eyes. "We were *acting*, darlin'."

"An Oscar-winning performance, no doubt," I said, my voice dripping with irony. But I felt myself soften to his touch. Was he telling the truth?

He laughed and pulled me close. "I certainly hope so. Sweetheart, can't you see what I'm trying to tell you? We were rehearsing because Caroline is so bloody stiff and cold in the love scenes. I just wanted her to relax. And we weren't naked, even if it must have looked like it in the photo. I had my pants on and she was in this flesh-coloured slip, or whatever you call it. The director was there, too, in the background, but you probably couldn't see him."

I sighed and relaxed in his arms, too tired to fight. "Okay," I whispered into his neck. "I believe you."

He pulled away and looked at me. "You do?"

I nodded and buried my nose in the hollow of his throat, breathing in the smell of soap and clean skin. "Yes."

"I could enquire about your hot date with that hunky farmer," Colin muttered. "You looked pretty cosy there, with your heads together, whispering and touching each other."

I sighed. "He was telling me about the woman he was in love with. His mother wouldn't approve, so they broke up."

Colin laughed softly. "A mammy's boy?"

"You could say that, yes. Not my kind of man, like you."

He held me tight. "What do we do now?"

"I don't know," I whispered. "Just keep holding me. I'm tired of being sad and lonely."

"Me too."

"What? You're sad and lonely? I find that rather hard to believe."

Colin took me by the arms and gave me a shake. "Oh, Finola, shut up, will ya? Why do you have to analyse everything I say? If I say I'm often sad and lonely, that's the truth."

"Okay."

"What do we do now? We can't stand here all night hugging."

I laughed, wiped my eyes and pulled away from his arms. I was going to say something, invite him to the cottage or tell him I'd go up to his room if he wanted that, when both our phones beeped at the same time. I glanced at mine. It was Audrey asking me to go to the office. I had to write that piece and do the whole coverage of Aidan's event for the following day's issue.

"Shit, I have to go and talk to the producer," Colin groaned as he looked at his phone. "Some problem with the schedule."

"And I have to go and make sure tomorrow's edition is okay. And write the article about the launch. I also have to check on the finals and the layout and stuff."

"So we'll have to put this—us—on hold, then," Colin said softly.

"I suppose," I sighed.

He touched my cheek. "I'll call in on you later. Would that be okay? I just want to talk to you."

I nodded. "Me too. About lots of things. Everything."

"Yes." Colin put his hands on my shoulders and looked at me. "Just remember this—I hate small talk. With you, I want to talk about death, aliens, sex, magic, intellect, the meaning of life, faraway galaxies, the lies you've told, your flaws, my flaws, your favourite colour, your childhood, what keeps you up at night, your insecurities, your fears. I like your depth and twisted mind. I don't want to know 'what's up,' or what the hell is 'trending' or whatever shit everyone else is talking about. Is that clear?"

"Completely," I laughed. "I'd love that. And I love you."

He looked at me, long and hard without speaking for what seemed like an hour. Had I said too much? Was this too heavy for him?

"Oh baby," he finally whispered and kissed the palm of my hand. Then he let me go and walked out.

CHAPTER 22

Needless to say, my mind wasn't entirely on the job as we toiled into the night to get the paper ready for printing in the early hours of the morning.

"How many copies should I say?" Mary asked as we got ready to send the thing off.

"Make it ten thousand," I said.

Audrey stared at me. "What? Ten thousand? That's nearly double our present circulation."

I nodded. "Yes, but we have late orders from shops in Michelstown and Cashel and Clonmel too. That new campaign is big news. Aidan said he'd been contacted by schools in those towns. They want him to go and speak to them."

"Wow. He's going to be famous. I saw the girls mob him outside the school hall."

I laughed. "Yeah, and he's loving it. Handles it well, too. He's only fourteen, but he's already developing a fan base."

"He has that Justin Bieber-Brad Pitt look that's so fab," Mary said dreamily.

"He gets it from his mother," Audrey said. "Gorgeous."

I shook my head. "Call me an old woman, but he's just a spotty, lanky teenager to me. But I see the potential, of course."

Audrey handed me a piece of paper. "Here, read this, old woman. It just came in so I printed it. An email from—"

"Oliver O'Keefe," I exclaimed. "What on earth?"
"Read it and find out," Audrey urged.
"Okay."

Dear Finola,

Congratulations on the excellent anti-bullying campaign! Great initiative.

I hope you don't mind me making a few suggestions to help raise money for further development of the website and the whole operation. I want to organise a charity walk between Cloughmichael and Cashel as soon as we can schedule it. I'd be happy to do all the publicity, and also print and distribute posters, flyers and forms for sponsorships. It'll be a 10-km walk, and we'll also have tea and cakes and local musicians and singers to perform at the end of the walk. It could be great family day out for everyone in the area. Let me know what you think, and contact me by replying to this email or calling my mobile number (see below)

All the best,
Oliver O'Keefe

My jaw dropped. "What? He wants to do all this?" Then I got it. "Of course, it's election year. This is a great way to cash in on what's trending right now. It's all a ploy to gain voters."

"Not only that," Audrey cut in. "There are whispers about town that his son is one of the bullies."

I looked at the email. "Yes. I know. So…this will make him look like goody two shoes and maybe squash the rumours about his son." I thought for a moment. "We can't get involved in this and neither should Aidan."

"Why?" Audrey asked. "Isn't it a great way to raise money for the campaign?"

I nodded. "Oh, yes, it would be. But it is also a ploy for O'Keefe to gain new voters. His name will be on every single flyer and poster. That's a sneaky way to raise awareness for his name."

"So what's wrong with that?" Mary asked, looking confused. "Oliver O'Keefe is an independent, isn't he?"

"Officially, yes." Suddenly drained, I sank down on a chair beside Mary's desk. "But I heard on the grapevine he's closely associated with the Irish Democrats. It's entirely possible he'll support them in every policy debate in the Irish parliament if he's re-elected."

"Oh." Audrey looked at me and nodded. "I see the problem now. But what are you going to do? I mean this looks like a lovely, generous offer. Won't it look bad if you say no?"

"Very bad," I agreed. "But I'm not going to say no *exactly*. I'm going to tell him we'll do it, but I won't tell him when until I find out the date of the election, which we'll know very soon. Then we'll do this charity walk afterwards."

Audrey looked awestruck. "That's bloody brilliant. It puts the onus on him to do it, but it won't give him the publicity he wants when he wants it."

I smiled. "That's right. But I won't tell him, of course. I'll just put it on the long finger. I'm going to talk to him right now. It's not too late, is it?"

Mary looked at her watch. "Ten thirty. Nah, I'm sure he's still up. He's probably waiting for you to call."

"Great." I grabbed the portable phone on her desk and dialled the number at the bottom of the email.

It didn't take long for a syrupy voice to reply. "Oliver O'Keefe."

"Hello there. Sorry to disturb you so late," I said. "This is Finola McGee."

"Good evening, Finola. Thank you for calling me back so promptly."

"You're welcome. Anyway," I breezed on, "I'd like to say a huge thank you for offering to organise this charity walk. It's a great idea and a very generous gesture."

"The least I could do. It's an important campaign. So we'll do it then?"

"Yes. I thought at the end of the summer?"

"Sounds good. You have a date in mind?"

"Not yet. I'll have to look at our schedule. We're busy with a magazine about the movie being made here, so maybe it would be better to have that out of the way first. You wouldn't want the event to be outshone by the Hollywood crowd and their publicity, would you?"

O'Keefe laughed heartily. "You're right there, darlin'. Let's see them off first. Then we'll get going on this. You'll put it on the front page? Photos and such?"

"Of course. We'll make sure it's the main event."

"That's perfect."

"I'll be in touch when we have decided on a date," I promised.

"Wonderful."

We said goodbye and I hung up, feeling only slightly guilty. "Okay, gang, what's left to do?" I said to Mary and Audrey, who were staring at me blankly.

Audrey snapped out of her trance. "We're nearly finished. Just a few adjustments and a correction to the piece about the event. I had Dan write it up, as you were part of the action, so to speak. And I knew you were busy. I found a few typos and one split infinitive."

"A split infinitive? Tsk, tsk," I said.

"Don't worry, I'll let him know." Audrey winked. "We'll finish here, if you want to get going."

"Thanks." I grabbed my things and shrugged on my jacket. "See you on Monday. Have a great weekend. Go easy on Dan, will ya, Audrey?"

"I'll coat it with sugar," she promised.

I laughed, waved, banged the door shut and ran down the steps, my heart beating and my head in the clouds, my meeting with Colin foremost in my mind. He'd said some things I couldn't forget. Surely this was meant to be, waiting to happen. I was no longer afraid to love someone. We might have a whole lifetime together or only a few days, it didn't matter. I knew this was it, the thing I'd been waiting for. Someone to love me.

* * *

I didn't notice them until I was nearly at the car—the shape of a group of people behind me. I thought they'd come out of the pub. But there wasn't the usual drunken banter between them, which was strange. They were silent, and as they drew closer, there was a palpable vibe of hatred. I glanced over my shoulder. There were three of them. I knew something was up and walked faster, holding onto my bag with hands that were suddenly clammy. My mouth dry, my heart beating, I stepped up the pace, but it was useless. They were faster, younger, stronger than me.

The street was so dark I couldn't see their faces, only hear their laboured breathing and smell sweat and beer. Then one of them shoved me sideways. I stumbled but managed to recover.

Then I was pushed again, and a voice behind me said, "Fucking blow-in bitch."

"Go back home, ya Dublin whore," another voice wheezed.

I was pushed yet again, harder this time. I fell, banging my elbow. I could see something being swung in the air. Then everything went black.

CHAPTER 23

A cold, damp cloth on my forehead. Fingers on my wrist. A searing pain in my head. I blinked against a bright light and closed my eyes again. Someone moaned.

"I think she's coming to," a voice said. "Can you hear me?"

"Yeah, yeah, I can hear you," I mumbled. "Shut up. My head hurts."

"What's your name?"

"Finola," I wheezed. "What's yours?"

"Finola what?"

I tried to laugh. "You're Finola too?" I opened my eyes again, looking at a pale, puffy face with small dark eyes that peered at me. A woman, judging by the hair tied back in a bun.

"No, *you* are Finola. But can you tell me your last name?"

"Jesus, you're very inquisitive. Okay, my name is Finola McGee, and I work at the…the newspaper."

"Which newspaper?"

I waved my hand at her. "You know, The…thingy. Knockmealdown News." I tried to sit up. "Feck! We were supposed to send the next edition to the printers."

Audrey's face came into view. "It's okay. All gone off. Don't worry, Finola."

I stared at her. "What are you doing here?" I looked around slowly and saw a curtain. "Where am I?"

"In Clonmel Hospital," Audrey said. "This is Soraya. She's a nurse."

"Oh." I put a hand to my head. "This is one hell of a hangover. What did I drink?"

"Nothing," Nurse Soraya said. "You were found on the street, beside your car."

"Who found me?"

"I did," Audrey replied. "I called an ambulance straight away. We think someone attacked you. Can you remember anything?"

I closed my eyes and tried to think. Cast my mind back to that dark street and shivered. "Shadows…shapes…there were three of them, I think. In dark clothes."

"Did you see any of them?" a male voice asked.

I opened my eyes and saw a young Garda looking at me. "No. Too dark. I could smell them though. Beer and BO. Vile. And they shouted abuse at me, and then I fell and something hit me on the head. I think I rolled sideways to avoid whatever it was. Looked like a hurling stick."

"You were lucky," Nurse Soraya said. She took the cloth off my forehead and put a clean compress on it. "You have nasty gash, but it could have been a lot worse."

"Do you want to report this?" the Garda asked.

"Sure I do," I mumbled. "But what can I say? I was attacked by dark shapes, who called me a fucking blow-in, pushed me down and hit me with a hurling stick. The End." I let out a long sigh and closed my eyes. "I want to go home. I want to sleep in my bed and wake up to the birds singing and the bees—"

"I'm afraid you have to wait here until you've been seen by a doctor," Nurse Soraya said. "He'll want to put stitches in and examine you."

"How long will that be?" I asked.

The nurse sighed. "Could be hours. This is one of the busiest nights of the week." She patted me on the shoulder.

"Try to rest, and then I'm sure the doctor will let you go home, unless he finds something seriously wrong with you." Something beeped. "Sorry, another ambulance coming in. I'll see you later." She pulled the curtain closed on my cubicle before she left.

"Anything else?" the Garda insisted. "Voices? Height, clothes, colour of hair?"

I shook my head, but stopped when the pain hit me. "No. Voices? Tipperary accents. You know, the way you say 'fock' around here? Clothes? Hoodies, I think. Height? Taller than me, about a head. So perhaps six foot or so. That's all I can remember."

"Young or old?" he asked.

I opened my eyes and glared at him. "It was as dark as the inside of a coal cellar. Not that I've ever been in one, but that's the idea. Got it? Now please, go away."

He nodded. "In a minute. Did they steal anything?"

"I don't know." I looked at Audrey. "Where's my bag?"

She held it up. "Here. And I checked. Your wallet is missing, but your keys are there."

"Weird," I mumbled.

"A personal attack with no apparent motive," the Garda mumbled, taking notes. "Theft of wallet with…" He looked at me. "How much was in it?"

"Twenty euros. Not much to worry about. But shit, my driving licence was in it."

"But I found your phone on the ground not far from your car," Audrey announced. She showed it to me.

I glanced at it. "That's not my phone. I have an iPhone. That's a—"

"Samsung Galaxy SX," Audrey said, glancing at it. "Could it belong to one of the—"

The Guard snatched the phone from her hand. "I'll take that. If one of your attackers dropped it, we might be able to identify him."

Audrey dug in my bag. "Your phone's here, actually. At the bottom of your bag."

"Oh, good. At least I have my phone." I closed my eyes and relaxed.

"I'll type up what you said, and then we'd appreciate it if you could come down to the station and sign it," the Garda said.

"Fine. I will when I get out of here." I waved my hand at him limply. "Now go and see if you can find me that doctor. I want to go home. This trolley is very uncomfortable."

"I'm afraid you'll have a long wait," the Garda said. "I've just seen the waiting room. Good luck." He nodded and left.

"Gee, thanks," I muttered. I touched the side of my head. The compress the nurse had put there was wet, and I could see blood on my hand when I removed it. "Where *is* that nurse? Audrey, could you see if you can find her? She'll need to do something about this."

Audrey jumped up from her chair and looked at my head. "God, yes, you're right. I'd better go and find you a doctor."

"A doctor?" I scoffed. "You might as well ask for champagne and caviar served by George Clooney."

"Just watch me," Audrey said and swished through the curtain on her high heels.

I closed my eyes and kept my hand pressed on the wound that seemed to be bleeding profusely. I'd never felt so alone in all my life. Why couldn't someone come and help me stem the blood? Would I bleed to death before anyone noticed me? Was this what they meant when they complained about our lousy health service?

To my relief, Audrey reappeared with a young man in blue scrubs wearing a stethoscope around his neck. "I caught one," she said triumphantly. "He was just coming out of theatre, so I nabbed him before he could run away."

The young man laughed. "Hi, I'm Doctor McNally. Your friend said you were haemorrhaging to death and she'd sue the pants off me if I didn't come and save you."

"Not quite haemorrhaging," I said. "But it looks pretty bad from my side."

He glanced at the side of my head. "Yes, I see what you mean. That needs a stitch. I'll just go and get a nurse to help, and we'll have you sewn up in no time."

"I'll go with you," Audrey offered. "I'm not letting you out of my sight until you've stitched Finola up."

Dr McNally laughed. "Let's go then, darlin'." He disappeared with Audrey behind him.

They reappeared only minutes later with a nurse holding a bowl with sutures and dressings. The nurse cleaned me up while the doctor snapped on a pair of gloves.

"I should perhaps give you a local, but this will only take a few seconds. Three to four stitches should do it."

Audrey took my hand. "Squeeze if it hurts too much."

"You might be sorry you said—" I shut my eyes, clenched my jaw and gripped Audrey's hand as the first stitch went in. She groaned softly but held my hand tightly. I let out a moan at the second stitch and squealed at the third. But then it was done.

The doctor stepped away, pulling off his gloves. "There. All done. Pretty good job, if I say so myself. There'll be no scar, I hope."

"Whatever," I mumbled. "Who cares about a scar on that part of the body?" I slowly let go of Audrey's hand. "Sorry if I squeezed to hard."

Audrey massaged her hand. "It's okay. I think I'll be able to use it in about a month."

The doctor nodded at the nurse. "Put a dressing on that and then take her to X-ray. If there's no damage, you can go home, if you can get someone to drive you. Just take it easy for a couple of days, and don't move around too much. Any dizziness or nausea?"

I moved my head. "No, just a splitting headache."

"We'll get you something for that." He beamed a smile at Audrey. "Bye for now. See you tomorrow night?"

Audrey batted her eyelashes. "Looking forward to it."

"You asked him out on a date?" I said when the doctor had left.

Audrey laughed. "I kind of said it would be nice to see him out of scrubs. And then he said he couldn't do that right now, but if we got to know each other better, he'd think about it. Cute, isn't he?"

"I didn't notice. But thanks for sacrificing your reputation for me."

"It was a real pleasure."

The curtain swished open, and two burly young men came into view. "We're taking you to X-ray," one of them said and started to wheel my trolley into the corridor.

"See you later," Audrey said. "I'll hold on to your bag and take you home when you get the all-clear."

"*If* I do," I muttered as my trolley started to move away.

The cheery nurse in the X-ray department helped me on to the stretcher under the X-ray camera. She put some kind of heavy blanket to cover my chest and abdomen. "It's a lead apron. Just in case," she said.

"Just in case of what?" I asked.

"In case you're pregnant, of course. Is there any chance of that, do you think?"

I was going to say not a chance in hell, but stopped myself and nearly fainted as I realised there was a chance, a small chance, but still…Colin and our night together swam into my brain and I wondered if…

"Better safe than sorry," I muttered.

When my head had been X-rayed at different angles, Audrey's dishy doctor came back.

"No sign of any damage. But the headache might be due to concussion. So, if your nice friend could help you home, you should rest for a couple of days and not drive or do any strenuous exercise for at least a week. If you feel any worse, dizzy or nauseous, come in and we'll do a scan. But I'd say you were lucky and you should be fine in a little while." He patted me on the shoulder. "Okay?"

"Brilliant," I muttered.

He nodded and left, walking swiftly on his rubber soles, the way hospital staff do.

Audrey helped me to her car and drove me back to the cottage, where she helped me get undressed and into bed with an ecstatic Jake burrowing in beside me.

"Your phone's been pinging like mad," she said. "Do you want to look at your messages?"

"No. I just want to sleep. It might be Colin, but he'll be here soon, anyway."

"Colin? Here?" Audrey squealed.

I winced. "Please. Don't shout."

"Oops." She put her hand on her mouth. "Sorry," she whispered. "But you and he are—?"

"I don't know," I sighed. "But I have a feeling…shh, don't tell anyone, okay?"

"My lips are sealed. But I'll be smiling all night."

"Good." I closed my eyes, enjoying the sheer bliss of being in my own bed. I barely registered Audrey tiptoeing out. Minutes later, I vaguely heard her talking to someone, but I couldn't summon up enough energy to listen. I drifted off, my arms around Jake and my dreams full of Colin.

* * *

The dawn chorus was in full swing when I heard the door creak and footsteps coming across the flagstones in the hall and up the stairs. Jake didn't open his eyes, but wagged his tail and made a little noise, settling again at the foot of my bed as Colin peeked in. I smiled and moved over, folding the duvet back. Colin removed his jacket, tee shirt and jeans and crawled in beside me.

"Sorry," he murmured into my hair as he held me from behind. "I should have been there with you. But I was stuck in a stupid Skype meeting. Then Audrey rang the hotel and told me what happened. She said you were asleep and not to disturb you." He touched the dressing on the side of my head. "Fucking bastards. What did they do to you?"

"Beat me up," I mumbled.

He squeezed me so tight I could hardly breathe. "And I wasn't there to help."

"They'd have beaten you up too. Please. Don't squeeze me so hard."

He loosened his grip and touched my hair. "Oh baby."

I normally hated men calling me baby. Cory used to, but I never liked it. But when Colin said it, I felt a curious spark. As if he cared for me in a very special way. I'd be his baby, his girl, his woman, anything as long as we were together.

"I'll be fine," I said. "Don't worry. Those creeps won't win and they know it. That's why they're so pissed off with me." A thought struck me. Something Audrey had said. Messages on my phone. What was that all about? Not Colin, so who?

"Get me my phone," I ordered.

Colin pulled away and sat up. "What? Where is it?"

I made a gesture towards the floor. "In my bag. There, somewhere."

Colin found my bag, pulled out my phone and handed it to me. "There. Sure you want to check your messages?"

I dug out my phone. "Yes, because I have this feeling..."

I was right. I had four messages, all from different numbers and all in varying degrees of abuse. The last one said, *Next time, you'll be dead, bitch.*

I showed them to Colin, who blanched. "Fucking hell. You have to report this to the police."

"What good will that do?" I smiled. "I have a better idea."

I quickly tapped in a reply to the last message. *I know who you are, and if you don't stop this, I'll tell.*

The reply was instant. *Who you gonna tell, bitch? The cops? Lol.*

"They're pretty sure of themselves, the little shits," I muttered as I tapped in my reply.

"What are you going to tell them?"

I showed him my reply. It said, *Your dad.*

There were no more messages.

"You are, without a doubt, the smartest woman I've ever met," Colin laughed, squeezing me tight again. "Who's the dad?"

"I'm not sure, but I think it's Oliver O'Keefe. And I think he doesn't have a clue what his son's up to, but if he did, he'd beat him to a pulp with his golf club."

"Maybe you should tell him anyway?"

"Nah, then I'll have blown it. Let the little gobshites sweat forever. In any case, one of them dropped his phone. The Guards have it. I'm sure it won't take them long to find the little shits. Just leave it to them."

"Good idea." Colin yawned. "Sorry. My eyes are closing. I think I'll have a little snooze. We can talk later."

"Sounds good," I mumbled. "Let's snooze."

"Just one thing," Colin mumbled. "I forgot to say…"

"Yes?"

"I love you, Finola." He fell asleep with his arms around me, breathing softly into my hair.

My eyes opened wide. I nudged him awake. "Say that again. I'm not sure you said what you said."

"But I did," he mumbled. "I do. Love you."

"Oooh. Good." I closed my eyes and pressed my back against him.

His arms around me and his breath in my ear, I dozed off and didn't wake up until the rain was smattering against the window.

CHAPTER 23

I was barely awake when I heard someone knocking softly on the front door. I sat up in bed, trying to gauge how I felt. The room didn't sway, and the pain in my head was only a soft throbbing, not even warranting a painkiller. Colin was still asleep, curled into a ball, hugging his pillow like a little boy, his long eyelashes fanned out across his cheeks, his mouth relaxed. I pulled the duvet over him, threw on my dressing gown and crept downstairs. Jake was already standing by the door, wagging his tail. Whoever was knocking had to be a friend.

I opened the door and peered out into the rain to discover Rory in an old waxed coat holding an umbrella over a pretty woman in a bright red jacket, skinny jeans and a wide-brimmed hat.

"Rory?" I exclaimed. "Hi, what are you—"

Rory gasped as he caught sight of me. "Bloody hell, Finola! What happened to you?"

I touched my face, realising I must have looked a fright. I glanced in the hall mirror and saw I had two black eyes as well as the big dressing taped to the side of my head. They'd even shaved the bit where they'd applied the stitches, which I hadn't noticed in my confused state. I backed away from the door.

"I had a bit of an accident last night. Long story. Come

The Blow-In

in out of the rain, anyway. I was just putting on the kettle." I smiled at the woman. "Sorry about this. You must be Anita."

The woman looked confused. "No, I'm Clodagh, Rory's sister. Hi, Finola."

"Oh, sorry." I shook her hand. "Hi, Clodagh." I pulled the dressing gown tighter around me and stepped aside to let them in. Jake milled around us, sniffing at the newcomer's legs and whining. I went into the kitchen and filled the kettle. Rory hung his wet jacket on a peg by the door and followed me in, taking out cups and a teapot from the cupboard beside the Aga.

Clodagh stood in the middle of the floor and looked around. "Lovely little kitchen. You've made it look really homely."

"Just a lick of paint and a new kitchen table." I filled Jake's bowl with dog food. "But that was Jules, not me. I'm not much of a homemaker, really."

Rory filled the teapot with hot water and put it on the table. "Let's sit down. Tell us what happened."

"I need something to eat first." I slathered butter on a slice of soda bread from the fresh loaf I found on the counter. "What time is it?"

"Coming up to eleven thirty," Rory replied. "Here." He poured tea into a mug and pushed it at me across the table.

"Thanks." I looked back at him, and then at Clodagh. "Before I go into what happened to me, tell me why you're here. You both look as if you're in the middle of some kind of argument."

"More like a feud." Clodagh took off her hat, letting her brown hair spill onto her shoulders.

"Sounds ominous." I took a bite of the bread.

Rory fiddled with a teaspoon. "It's my mother. And me. I told Clodagh all about Anita and how Mam behaved towards her and how it made her break up with me. And then—"

"Then I got mad and decided to come here and tell Mam

where to get off," Clodagh cut in. "She seemed to think she has the right to decide everything on the farm and to kick Rory out if she feels like it. But she doesn't. Not legally, anyway. She owns two thirds and we own a third. We have a right to live in the house and to take part in the running of the land and livestock. But if Rory isn't there to keep an eye on things, God only knows what Mam will get up to. Now she's said Rory can't bring a woman into the house without her approval."

"And I told her I'd leave if I couldn't choose who I'd marry," Rory filled in.

I put a hand to my head. "This is getting complicated. What are you going to do?"

"Leave," Rory said.

"You can't," Clodagh argued. "Then one of us has to come and live with Mam, and you know that's not possible. Especially not for me."

I shook my head as I looked at them. "You know what? I think you should sort this out yourselves. I can't do it for you. Nobody can. I have a feeling Breda has been treating you like children all this time. Why don't you grow up and tell her where to get off? She's a bully, and like all bullies, she's a coward deep down. Go and find out for yourselves."

Rory looked at me as if I'd just dropped a bomb in his lap. He got up from the table, his face red. "You're right, Finola. We'll have to stand up for our rights. Come on, Clodagh, let's go."

Clodagh looked suddenly frightened. "What are we going to do, Rory?"

"I'm going to win," he said. "And you're going to help me. Hell, I spent ten years in politics. I should be able to tell my mother where to get off."

"Politics is a breeze compared to the mammy from hell," I remarked.

"But now the worm is turning," Rory said. "Come on, Clodagh, let's get going."

"Okay," Clodagh said in a small voice and got up. She turned to me. "I left home five years ago when I'd had enough of Mam breathing down my neck. I said I wouldn't set foot in the house until she was dead. Pretty harsh, but I was desperate. But now Rory needs help, so I'll try to…"

She was interrupted by Colin coming into the kitchen wearing nothing but a towel around his waist.

Looking startled, Rory stared at Colin, letting his gaze wander to the towel, then to me. "Is this the guy who beat you up, Finola?"

I dropped my mug. "What are you talking about?"

Rory pointed at Colin. "Him. And you with your face a mess. He did it, didn't he? I've heard about those Hollywood stars. Drugs, booze, fights…"

Colin stared at him. "You stupid bastard."

Rory took a step towards Colin, his fists clenched. "If you've hurt Finola, I'll—"

"NO," I shouted. "Colin didn't beat me up. He wasn't even there. It happened outside the office late last night. Some thugs pushed me around and then hit me with something and ran away."

Rory stopped and blinked. "Who?"

I shrugged. "No idea. But I have my suspicions. It was connected to the anti-bullying campaign. I spent a few hours at the hospital, and then I came here. And then…Colin…he and I…"

"Oh?" Rory said, looking sheepish. "I see. Sorry."

"Yeah." Colin backed away, holding his towel in a tight grip.

Clodagh suddenly woke up and pointed a shaking finger at him, her eyes on stalks. "It's Colin Foley! Naked in your kitchen! Where's my phone?"

"No, you don't." Colin backed out of the kitchen and disappeared up the stairs like a rocket.

Clodagh sighed. "He got away." She turned to me, her

eyes shining. "Finola, you're…I don't know what to say."

"Then don't," I snapped. "I'd appreciate it if you could keep who and what you saw here confidential. I'm sure the news about us won't take long to hit the tabloids, but until then it would be nice to have some privacy." I drew breath.

"Every woman in the world will want to be you when this comes out," Clodagh sighed.

I rolled my eyes. "Being me is no picnic at the best of times. So, I repeat, not a word for now, okay?"

"Of course," Rory said. "We know how to keep a secret, don't we, Clodagh?"

"Yeah, right," she muttered. "Don't worry. I'll keep my big mouth shut. Come on, Rory, let's go and deal with Mam."

Rory nodded and put on his jacket. Clodagh shoved her hat back on her head and grabbed the still-dripping umbrella. I went with them into the hall to see them out.

Rory put his hand on my shoulder. "Bye for now, Finola. And thank you. I'd never have the guts to stand up to my mother if you hadn't come along and shaken me up. Things are going to be different from now on."

"Good for you, Rory. Nice to meet you, Clodagh." I opened the door to make them leave.

"Fantastic to meet *you*," Clodagh replied, hovering on the doorstep. "You're even more amazing than I thought. I mean…Colin Foley."

"Yeah, okay. But please, could you leave so I can close the door? It's wet and cold out there." I shooed them both out the door and slammed it shut, leaning against it. "That was one crazy morning," I said to Jake. "Politicians are easier to handle."

I caught sight of my face in the mirror and shuddered. No wonder Rory got a fright. I sighed, suddenly too tired to move. I needed to sleep for at least a month.

Colin came down the stairs again, dressed in boxers and a tee shirt. He caught sight of me and rushed to my side.

"You need to get back into bed. Come on, sweetheart, I'll help you up the stairs."

"I hope you're strong enough," I mumbled and leaned heavily against him.

"Don't worry. I work out regularly." He took a firm grip around my waist, and I looped my arm around his shoulder. We managed to get up the narrow stairs and into the bedroom, where we collapsed on the bed.

Colin ran his finger down my face. "Did I tell you that I love you?"

I managed a smile. "Mm. You did."

"Good."

My phone beeped.

"Jesus Christ, not those gobshites again," Colin groaned. "Don't reply."

But I couldn't help myself. I had to reply. "Hello?" I squawked into the phone. "If you're calling to harass me, I'll—"

"Finola McGee?" A gravelly voice interrupted. "This is Garda Flannigan. I'm calling to let you know that we have arrested two men suspected of the assault on your…person."

I shot up from the bed. "Holy mackerel! You haven't!"

"We have," Garda Flannigan said, a hint of a smile in his voice. "One of them is the owner of the phone we found, and the other was caught trying to break into a house about an hour after your attack. We found your wallet among his belongings. They'll both be charged and held in custody."

I sat down heavily on the bed. "That is the best news ever. Well done, Mr Garda Flannigan! Who are these guys?"

"I'm not at liberty to say," Garda Flannigan said. "But we'll make a statement as soon as we can. You'll be the first to know."

"Fantastic," I gushed. "Thank you for letting me know."

"You're welcome. Bye for now, Miss McGee," Garda Flannigan said and hung up.

"What was that all about?" Colin demanded.

I beamed at him. "That was the Guards. They got the bastards."

Colin brightened. "Brilliant! Three cheers for the boys in blue." He pulled me down beside him. "But let's get back to where we broke off. Where were we…oh yes. I love you, Finola McGee."

"You love me even though I look like shit right now?"

He opened my dressing gown and buried his face in my chest. "I love you to bits whatever you look like. I want to be in your space, in your heart, in your mind." He kissed my breasts. "But most of all, right now, I want to be inside your body. But you're exhausted. Maybe we'll sleep on it?"

Despite my fatigue, the contact with his warm skin through the thin tee shirt and his mouth on my breasts made something stir deep down inside me. I suddenly wanted him so much it hurt.

"I'm wide awake," I whispered and ran my hands under his tee shirt, all the way down to his crotch, where something was beginning to rise. I pulled him on top of me and arched my hips, undulating my pelvis, parting my legs.

"No headache?" he whispered as he slid inside me.

"Just a throbbing, but that's not in my head."

And then we made love. Slowly at first, building up to a crescendo that made the bed shudder and shake. We moaned in unison, and came at the very same time, eyes locked, our breathing sounding like some kind of electronic music from a sci-fi movie.

He pulled away, smiling and sighing at the same time. "Finola, you're amazing."

I touched his face. "No, we're amazing. Together." I gasped, suddenly remembering something. "Shit, we did it again."

"Yes, we did. Why do you look so startled?"

"I mean we had sex without…without a net."

He frowned. "You mean without protection?"

"Yes, that's what I meant. How could we be so stupid?"

"Stupid? Yeah, I suppose…" He sat up and stared out the window at the rain. Then he looked back at me. "How would you feel if…?"

I thought about it for a minute. "Shocked. But then happy. It would change my life forever."

"And mine." He kept looking at me. "You don't think I'd run off if you got pregnant?"

"I don't know what you'd do. I was hoping not, but…" I thought about it for a while. "It was my responsibility, too. I could have said no, I could have asked you if you had a condom, I could have had one myself, except I don't keep them in stock because I don't have sex that often. It's been a while, you know," I ended, and started to cry for no reason.

Colin lay down beside me and held me tight. "Let's get married."

I stopped crying. "What?"

"Yeah, let's do it. Let's go up the aisle and do it properly. A real, big, fat, Irish wedding. Church, priest, bridesmaids, flowers, everyone crying and…"

I couldn't believe it. "You want that? But you were married before. I don't think the Catholic Church will marry us on those grounds."

He laughed. "That wasn't real. We were married in The Chapel of Love in Las Vegas, by a guy dressed like Elvis. The witness was an old woman with pink hair they got off the street. I think she was drunk. So was the bride. We split up after three weeks. The whole thing was a joke. I bet the marriage wasn't even legal."

"Did you love her?" I had to ask.

He shrugged. "Nah. I thought I did, but it was when I was drinking quite a lot. I didn't feel like I feel now about you." He picked up my hand and kissed it. "You're my Dublin girl. You know where I'm coming from. I'm gonna get you the biggest rock you've ever seen. And then we'll plan the wedding."

"Oh, God. Is this happening?"

"No, it's a dream. I ordered it especially for you." He got off the bed and held out his hands. "Come on, let's have a shower. Then you're going back to bed, and I'll make us something to eat. I got some fresh bread at the all-night shop on the motorway."

I got off the bed. "And there are eggs and bacon in the fridge."

"Perfect."

Colin helped me into the shower and washed me as tenderly as if I was a baby. Then I sank into bed and fell asleep, waking up to the smell of bacon frying and crockery rattling in the kitchen. I heard Colin talking to Jake, and smiled to myself. I knew we wouldn't be the perfect couple and that our careers and lifestyles would never really gel. There would be rocky patches along the way, fights, separations, compromises. I was certain of nothing except one thing. We would never stop loving each other.

EPILOGUE

Oliver O'Keefe's son was charged with assault, along with the son of a former Garda. The news made the headlines the following week, which should have made me very happy. But by then I had other things on my mind.

I knew it would happen, we both did. We didn't talk about it until it was confirmed by that little blue line on the stick of the pregnancy test I got at the pharmacy in Cork. I drove all the way there to buy one where nobody would know or care who I was.

We sat on my bed early one morning and stared at that little stick, both holding our breaths. Then it showed positive. I couldn't move or breathe. There it was: clear, cold proof of what we had been half hoping, half fearing. A new life inside me. Something that would one day be someone—a human being that would change both our lives forever.

I looked at Colin's shocked face. He was as white as a sheet. "Bloody hell," he whispered. "I'm going to be a dad."

"Looks that way, yes," I said.

He took my hand. "You're ice cold. Are you as scared as I am?"

"Terrified," I whispered.

"And excited? I am. What an adventure it'll be. Bringing up a kid. Being parents, a family." He sighed and smiled. "We'll do it. Together."

I couldn't help smiling. "Yes, we will. And we have a little time to prepare and plan. But first we have to get through the cast party and the launch of the magazine in a few days."

"And the wedding? You have to marry me now, you know." He kissed my hand. "Please, please say yes this time. I don't want my son to be a—"

"Or daughter," I interrupted.

"Yes, yes, or daughter. Whatever it is, the kid won't thank you for not making me respectable."

I sighed. "Oh, okay then. I'll marry you."

He squeezed my hand and tumbled me down on the bed. "Finally! Jesus, you're one stubborn woman."

I touched his face. "I know, but…oh, I don't want a big splashy wedding."

"What? And I had this dream of getting married Hollywood-style in Marbella and selling the rights to the pictures to Hello Magazine. I see you floating down the aisle in a dream by Dior."

I bashed a pillow into his face. "Shut up!"

Colin laughed and hit me back with the pillow. "I don't give a damn how we do it as long as we do it. Don't know how we're going to keep away the sharks though. I mean the media sharks."

"Leave it to me. I think I know how to get us married without any fuss."

I got to work the next day and went to have a chat with the parish priest in the little village down the road from the cottage. I came clean about not being much of a mass-goer and that my faith was less than solid. I also told him of Colin's first marriage that wasn't real but still some kind of relationship. Father Bob smiled benignly and said the church would never turn away a lost sheep. And two lost sheep wanting to get married in God's house would pose no problem at all. But we had to do a marriage course, which consisted of an hour or two of pleasant chats about marriage, parenthood and Catholic family life.

"Not too scary at all," Colin declared afterwards as we walked back to the cottage. "We didn't even have to swear to stick to those rules."

"But you'll have to stick to the wedding wows," I argued. "Till death do us part. Are you sure you want to stand in front of a priest and several witnesses and promise all that?"

"I've never been surer. But you didn't tell me how we'd do this wedding."

I told him. It would be small, simple and secret. No photographers, except Dan with his precious camera. The news would break the next day, but then we would be far away, on honeymoon in a secret spot: Ahakista, that remote village on the edge of Ireland. I had already booked a week in a holiday cottage there.

Colin agreed to it all without blinking. "That's the least difficult part. But when the news about us being married comes out, there'll be a whole new ball game. We'll be followed around by photographers for the next few years, as long as my career holds. Pictures of us arguing, of us kissing, of us naked will appear in the gossip press. Rumours will fly. Every time one of us appears near someone else of the opposite sex, there will be talk of a rift, of 'marriage problems', or even imminent divorce. Are you ready for that?"

I laughed. "I know what journalists are like. I can take it, don't worry."

"We have to make plans," Colin said, looking worried. "Where do we live, what will happen to your career, or mine."

I stopped walking. "I have been thinking about that. A lot. Obviously, you can't live with me here in the cottage while I run The Knockmealdown News."

He laughed. "No, babe, I'm afraid not. But you in LA? I can't quite picture you on Rodeo Drive in stilettoes, shopping and having coffee with your girlfriends."

"Damn right you can't," I agreed. "That's not going to happen. But there must be more to LA than that. I know that workwise, I can freelance. Maybe report on American politics for Irish newspapers. I've already been in touch with The Examiner and The Indo. I think one of them might bite. So I'll work from home, wherever your home is. Where in LA is it?"

"Malibu," Colin mumbled. "Yeah, I know, it's the fashionable place to live. But I hate it. Thought we could sell up and move to somewhere quiet nearby. But for now, I'm right on the beach behind high walls, but with great views of the ocean. Not the greatest place for kids, but…"

I put my hand on my stomach. "I'm sure the baby will be happy wherever we are for the first year or so. Don't panic, sweetheart, we'll be okay. I'll come to LA as soon as I've settled things here. Jerry won't be happy when I tell him I'm leaving."

"Maybe Johnny Keegan could come back now that the bullies have been caught?" Colin suggested.

I sighed. "That would be perfect. But not possible. I already spoke to Johnny and, even though he was pleased to hear about the arrests, he said he and Madlena were so happy in Ahakista and Drago loves it so much. There's no way they'll ever leave. But I have an idea…"

"Tell me."

"Audrey. She could run the paper with both hands tied behind her back, metaphorically speaking. I've never met anyone so clued into journalism and marketing. All I have to do is convince Jerry."

"Sounds like a good choice. But what about Jake?" Colin asked, a note of panic in his voice.

"I'll have him microchipped, and he'll be one of those VIP pooches who travel with their owners wherever they go."

"Great. You'll have to wrap things up here before you can think of moving anyway."

I nodded. "Yes. I have to give in my notice and settle

Audrey into the job, and—" I stopped, tears stinging my eyes.

Colin stared at me. "What's wrong?"

I started walking again, turning my face away. "I know it's silly, but…I suddenly felt so sad about leaving this place—this little cottage, the town and all the people I've made friends with in such a short time."

He put his arm around my shoulders and fell into step beside me. "You can come back here as often as you want. Why don't we make this our Irish base? Tell Jules we'd like to have the cottage on a long lease. I'm sure she'll be happy not to have to go through the hassle of letting it again."

I punched him on the shoulder. "There you go with your magic wand again. Solving everything by throwing money around."

He pulled away. "You don't like that idea?"

"I love it, you eejit. It's just that I find it odd to have someone else taking charge. I've always been my own boss."

Colin put up his hands. "You can be my boss too, if you want. I love domineering women."

"Then you've truly struck gold." We'd reached the front gate to Jules's property. "Come on, let's go and tell Jules."

Colin stopped me. "But the ring. Don't forget the ring. I don't know what kind of engagement ring you want."

I laughed. "Surprise me."

* * *

And he did. The ring was presented to me just before we left for the big party at The Bianconi Inn. A pear-shaped-cut diamond glinting in a blue velvet box. Big, flashy, vulgar—and totally irresistible.

I stared at it, speechless.

Colin, devastating in a tux, laughed and pushed it on the

third finger of my left hand. "There. We're officially engaged."

I couldn't take my eyes off it. "Holy shit," I exclaimed. "It's…it's…huge."

"Suits you."

I spread out my fingers and held my hand out. "Hmm. Not sure. Must have cost a—"

Colin's mouth on mine silenced me. "Yes, it did, but as they say in those ads, you're worth it."

"Feck off!" But I couldn't stop looking at it. God, I adored it. It was as if Colin's love for me was in every facet of that diamond, glinting back at me.

"We can change it for something else," Colin mumbled.

I looked at him. "Are you kidding? I'll never take it off."

"Thank God for that. Jesus, you're one difficult, complicated woman. But I love you."

I grinned. "Me too. You. Would you call this a happy ending?"

"No. But maybe a happy beginning?" He took my hand. "Let's go to the party and show off."

THE END

Acknowledgements

I would like to express my appreciation to my terrific beta readers who so kindly read through the book in its various stages of production. Many thanks, Korine Brooks Keith, Andrea Emm, Win Johnson, Vickie Greupink Boehnline and my super-beta-editor Cathy Speight. I couldn't have done this without you!

Thanks also to the wonderful members of the Writers' Pub, who are always there if I need a helping hand, advice and support. And of course, my street team, who cheer me on and help to spread the word about my books around the Internet!

Last but not least, I must thank Jane Dixon-Smith of JD Smith Design for yet again, a wonderful cover.

About the author

Susanne O'Leary is the bestselling author of twenty novels, mainly in the romantic fiction genre. She has also written three crime novels and two in the historical fiction genre. She has been the wife of a diplomat (still is), a fitness teacher and a translator. She now writes full-time from either of two locations, a ramshackle house in County Tipperary, Ireland or a little cottage overlooking the Atlantic in Dingle, County Kerry. When she is not scaling the mountains of said counties, practising yoga, or keeping fit in the local gym, she keeps writing, producing a book every six months.

Look up Susanne's website for more details about her work: http://www.susanne-oleary.co .uk

Printed in Great Britain
by Amazon